"Do you v⎯⎯⎯⎯⎯ he asked, his ⎯⎯⎯⎯⎯ ire and other e⎯⎯⎯⎯⎯ n't quite label.

Or maybe he didn't want to quite yet.

The steam from the hot water floated around her body, giving the illusion that she was hovering on a cloud.

Ivy shook her head and then looked at him. There was no anger, no fury in those eyes. He saw loss and pain and a vulnerability he'd never thought to see in her.

He stared at her, feeling like a cad for drinking in his fill of her incredible body, but she made no move to cover herself or to pull the curtain shut.

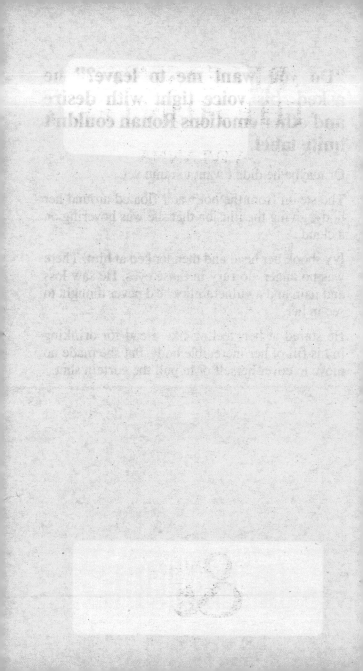

RELEASING
THE HUNTER

VIVI ANNA

First published in Great Britain 2013
by Mills & Boon, an imprint of Harlequin (UK) Limited,
Eton House, 18-24 Paradise Road, Richmond, Surrey TW9 1SR

© Vivi Anna 2013

ISBN: 978 0 263 90413 0
ebook ISBN: 978 1 472 00677 6

089-0913

Printed and bound in Spain
by Blackprint CPI, Barcelona

A vixen at heart, **Vivi Anna** likes to burn up the pages with her original, unique brand of fantasy fiction. Whether it's in the Amazon jungle, an apocalyptic future or the otherworld city of Necropolis, Vivi always writes fast-paced action-adventure with strong independent women that can kick some butt, and dark delicious heroes to kill for.

Once shot at while repossessing a car, Vivi decided that maybe her life needed a change. The first time she picked up a pen and put words to paper, she knew she had found her heart's desire. Within two paragraphs, she realized she could write about getting into all sorts of trouble without suffering any of the consequences.

When Vivi isn't writing, you can find her causing a ruckus at downtown bistros, flea markets or in her own backyard.

To all those who battle the dark forces
and keep us safe.

Chapter 1

The *thump thump thump* of hip-hop music vibrated over Ivy Strom's flesh, making the little hairs on her arms stand to attention. The rhythmic noise was so loud she could barely hear her own rapid heartbeat.

She took another sip of her tonic and lime, the liquid quenching her dry throat. From her perch on the stool at the main bar, she scanned the dance floor once more for her quarry, her eyes pausing every so often on lone males.

She'd been told that Sallos, the Great Duke of Hell, would be here, lurking around like the degenerate demon he was. He'd taken two girls from here in the past four months. This was supposedly one of his favorite hunting grounds.

Now it was hers.

Ivy shifted in her seat; the silver daggers she had strapped to her sides underneath her T-shirt were starting to chafe. It was difficult to dress inconspicuously for a club and still carry as much hardware as she wanted.

She had no less than four knives on her, all silver; two ampuls of holy water, hidden carefully in her cleavage; and she'd hung a bag of salt from her belt. And of course she wore a blessed silver cross around her neck. She was prepared for anything to happen. With demons, it usually did.

She'd been hunting this one for a little over five months now. For the past year he'd been terrorizing the streets of San Francisco. Seven women had been murdered so far. They'd all been identified by their dental records and fingerprints. Because this demon didn't leave much to recognize.

But his reign was over as far as Ivy was concerned. She'd gotten a reliable tip that he'd be here at this club tonight and Ivy was ready for him. She'd take him out, but not before she got a chance to interrogate him. It was her job to hunt him down, but there was also a personal reason behind her need to find him. This demon supposedly had information that could locate Quinn Strom, Ivy's brother.

He'd been missing for three years now. He was the last of her family and she swore she'd never give up searching until she found him, dead or alive. At least then she'd know, and she could move on with her life. Or exact her revenge, which would be more like it. The Stroms were all about revenge and justice.

She'd been born into the hunting community. Her dad had been a hunter when he'd met her mother. He'd actually met her while chasing down a rogue priest who'd been possessed by a strong wrath demon. Ivy's mother had been in the wrong place at the wrong time, but her father had saved her life before the demon could do any permanent damage.

They never married, but they lived together, and she had learned the ways of the hunter. She had Quinn shortly after, then Ivy two years later. She'd died when Ivy was only nine. On the job, of course. It had always been about the job. Usually just their dad would go out on hunts, for days sometimes. But on a few occasions, both parents went. In this particular case, Quinn had been left to take care of her while their mom and dad hunted. Dad had come back alone.

Hunters rarely lived to a ripe old age.

Ivy ran a hand over the cross at her throat. The necklace had been a gift from Quinn about a month before he disappeared. When he gave it to her, he told her never to remove it. It would protect her day and night from everything, including the nightmares she sometimes had. After he left, she never did take it off. It was her last reminder of him. Everything else he had taken with him, wherever that was.

She missed him. When he disappeared it was as if he taken a part of her with him. They'd been close. Had to be to endure the constant moving around the country and their dad's long absences while he hunted. Quinn had never let her out of his sight. He'd always been there for her. When she'd have nightmares, which was often, he'd be there to soothe her back to sleep. In many ways, Quinn had raised her. Not her dad.

Then he'd vanished and she'd been left to pick up the pieces of her life and of the hunt.

She finished her drink and slid off her stool. She'd do a walk around the club. There were some dark areas that she couldn't quite see from the bar. This was where she could rely on the amulet she wore around her neck to help her search. When a demon was near, it lit up with a blue glow somewhat like a firefly. It heated up as well, so she'd feel it against her skin instantly if a demon crossed her path.

Brushing past some enthusiastic dancers, Ivy circled the dance floor. It was crammed with gyrating sweaty young people of every race and sexual orientation. As she moved past, she almost got swept up in the soulful throb of the music. The primal beats thumped in time to her heartbeat and she found she had to force herself not to move her body to the electrifying rhythm. On another night, she might've indulged. It had been too long since she'd had any sort of fun.

Because demon hunting had been part of her life since childhood, she'd been homeschooled so the family could travel often. So she'd never had those lifelong school friendships. In fact, she'd never had a real friend until she grew up and went out on her own. Even now, she had to keep her distance from people. She could never get too close in case she had to flee at the last second.

It was a rough life, but one she'd been born into. It suited her in many ways and she couldn't imagine doing anything else.

She'd done one sweep of the club and was about to go back to her seat at the bar when the amulet flared to life. Instantly, it was hot.

He was near. Close to her.

She stopped and eyed the dancing crowd. She'd

know him the second she saw him. After years of hunting demons, she knew the signs to look for. Signs the regular folk mistook for dark and dangerous allure. To Ivy it was just dark and dangerous. Nothing alluring whatsoever.

She saw him. He was dancing with two young blondes. He was tall, with longish blond hair, not handsome or ugly. Average, mostly. Like a wolf in sheep's clothing. But it was the eyes that gave him away. When he turned ever so slightly to the left or the right, Ivy could see the flames in his soul.

The unholy fire that he carried within from the depths of hell.

She stepped onto the dance floor. She had to separate him from the women. If he spotted her now, he'd have no qualms about killing them right there and then.

Picking up the rhythm, Ivy danced her way through the writhing crowd. She tried not to stare directly but she needed to keep her eye on him. If she lost him now, it would take months to pick up his trail again. And more women would die. She'd already blown three previous tips because of her impatience. Something she should have grown out of years ago.

As she moved through the throng of people, someone grabbed her rear end. She stopped to glare at the guilty party. He had the presence of mind to turn and leave immediately. People didn't usually mess with Ivy, and if they did it was only once. She didn't suffer fools easily.

She had a reputation for being cold as steel and just as inflexible. This was probably why she didn't have a man or even bothered to date. What man could possibly live up to any of her expectations or abide by her rules of conduct?

None that she'd met so far.

The song changed tempo. The demon wrapped his arms around the two women and they slow danced together. His back was to her, which afforded her an opportunity to walk right up to him. And she did.

She tapped him on the shoulder. He turned and smiled at her. She tried to keep her face unreadable, a mask of indifference, when really she fumed with rage just being next to him.

"Can I cut in?" she asked with a grin she hoped was sexy and not laced with fury.

He looked her up and down. "Sure, Snow White."

She got that comment a lot. It was because of her chin-length jet-black hair and pale complexion. To top it off, she'd chosen a perfect shade of red for her lips. Demons were attracted to the fiery color. Probably reminded them of home sweet home.

She smiled at him and let him put his hands on her tiny waist.

The other two women sneered at her. She sneered right back and said, "You can get lost now. The main attraction's arrived."

They stomped off the dance floor.

One goal down, one more to go. She needed to get him outside so she could stun him with the holy water and salt. Then she'd take him somewhere she could bind him in a devil's trap and ask him questions. After he told her what she needed to hear she would slide her long silver blade through his heart. Or throat. Either spot would do to kill him and send him back home.

Ivy moved a little closer to him, trying hard not to cringe, and said, "Let's get out of here. My car is parked in the alley."

He grinned at her, and then leaned down to her ear. "Sure, Ivy. I'd love to."

Grinding her teeth, she took a step back from him.

"I saw you the second you walked into the club." He still danced in front of her, wriggling his hips seductively. "A guy just can't miss that devastating face and killer body. Get it, killer?" He licked his lips.

"What now?" she asked. She didn't want to make a scene. He had the upper hand here. He knew she wouldn't want him to do anything rash and start killing people.

"We could still go out back and get our groove on. I wouldn't mind tapping that ass of yours."

Her fingers were itching to reach under her shirt and pull out her blades. She wondered if she could instead reach for the holy water and splash him with it. It might be enough to subdue him so she could take him out. Except the crowd was pushing in on her and she had barely enough room to shift from foot to foot.

"I'm going to kill you." She flashed him a big grin and as quick as she could reached into her cleavage and plucked out an ampul.

But he was quicker.

He pushed her into the crowd. She stumbled backwards, knocking over two people. By the time she righted herself, he was on the move.

He crossed the dance floor in seconds and made his way to the back of the club, shoving people to the side as he dashed past. Ivy followed him, trying not to ram into the same people in his wake.

She thought about unsheathing her knives, but knew it would be risky inside the club with so many people around. What if someone accidentally ran into her? There were no take backs in demon hunting. When a blade went in, that was it. There was no second chance. Her knives were lethally sharp, coated with salt and blessed by a priest. They were meant to kill. Demon or human, the result was usually the same.

He ran past the washrooms and through the kitchen. He was heading for the back door, that much she knew. She tried to keep up as best she could, but demons were fast and light on their feet. She'd even seen some run up walls and jump over cars. Agility was their strong suit.

Ivy weaved around the baffled kitchen staff; some were pointing to the back, cursing up a storm at having been interrupted. At least she knew which way the demon went.

The back door had just finished swinging when she pushed through it, one hand already snaking up her torso to snag a blade.

The second she was out the door, she hit a wall. Well, not a real wall, but a man built like a brick house.

She bounced off his chest and landed on her butt on the ground.

He reached down with his hand to help her up. "Are you okay?"

She took it and let him heave her to her feet, but she quickly let it go when she realized how hot her chest was getting. She glanced down and saw the glow of her amulet. It lit up the alleyway in blue.

"Damn it." She reached into her shirt and

grabbed her last ampul. Setting it in the palm of her hand, she smashed it against the man's chin, then reaching down for her salt bag, she untied it and quickly dashed salt all over his head.

She stood back waiting for the wailing and the skin bubbling to begin. But nothing happened.

He just looked at her, a rather pissed-off look in his eyes, then wiped at the water dripping off his chin. The glass of the ampul made a nick in his skin. Blood beaded to the surface. He dabbed at it with his thumb.

"You're not melting."

He ran a big hand through his tousled dark hair, and then said, "Yeah, about that."

Chapter 2

Ronan Ames knew exactly who he was standing in front of. Ivy Strom was legendary. Especially in the demon world. She looked exactly how everyone described her.

Gorgeous, with silky black hair, luminous blue eyes and a dynamite body, but as cold and razor-sharp as icicles.

She'd removed one of her blades and had it pressed against his neck. "Are you a demon?"

He had to think about his answer. Because he knew if he gave her the wrong one, she'd slide that blade right into his throat.

"No," he said, and then added, "Not really."

She frowned, pressing the tip into his flesh. "Is it no, or not really?"

"It's complicated."

"Well, you better explain it before I run you through."

"How about lowering the knife, and then I *will* explain." He put his hands out to the side to show her that he wasn't holding a weapon. He had a bunch strapped to his body, though, but he didn't need to tell her that.

Ice-blue eyes narrowing, she lowered the knife and took a step back. He noticed she made no move to sheath her blade. He wasn't surprised. She was infamous for being cautious to the point of paranoia. Probably how she'd stayed alive so long.

"Speak."

He lowered his hands. "Before I tell you, I want you to know that I am not your enemy and, in fact, we are after the same demon."

She cocked one eyebrow but remained silent, waiting for him to continue.

"I have demon blood in my veins."

She flinched, and her blade came up.

But he was prepared this time.

He blocked her arm and quicker than she could see he grabbed her other arm, swung her around and pressed her tight to his body, effectively pinning both arms to her sides.

She struggled against him, cursing up a storm. There were even a few choice words he'd rarely heard before, especially from female lips.

"Stop," he grunted. "I told you, I am not your enemy."

"Then why are you restraining me?" She tried to dig her boot heel into his shin, but he moved his leg in time.

"Because you're trying to hurt me."

That seemed to give her pause and she ceased struggling.

With her still in his arms, he became acutely aware of her tantalizing scent and the way her hard body fit against his. Heat from her form spilled over onto him and sent a ripple of pleasure over him.

Ivy Strom was enticing to say the least, distracting at most. Just from their brief struggle, he could tell how strong she was, how agile and fierce. He didn't have to see under her clothes to know that she'd be well muscled and toned. The delectable swell of her behind rubbed him in all the right places at definitely the wrong time.

Despite his demon blood, he was also a man, and he couldn't help his reaction to her.

She must've noticed because she shook her head and growled, "Release me now. Before I cut it off."

Ronan released her, pushing her forward and

taking a distancing step away. "I apologize. It's just you're, ah, attractive."

She smirked. "And you're obviously still in high school."

He gave her a small smile. "Evidently."

Her lips twitched at that, but she fought it before they could form a smile. He did notice the playful glint in her piercing eyes, though. Interesting. Something he might have to consider later.

"So you're a cambion," she said.

He shrugged. "Yeah. My lot in life."

"I've heard of them existing. But it's pretty rare. Don't most die when going through the transformation?"

"Yup. I didn't. Lucky me."

She studied him for a moment, and then shook her head in anger. "Yeah, well, thanks to you, I lost my mark." She sheathed her blade. "I'm going to have a hell of a time finding him again."

"I think I can help with that."

She eyed him warily. "How?"

"I know where he lives."

"Where?"

He shook his head. "It's not going to be that easy. I want to team up with you."

"Forget it." She turned to go, but he grabbed her arm. She glared down at his hand.

"We're both after the same thing. Makes sense to team up."

"Maybe to you, but not to me." She lifted her gaze to his. It was intense and fierce and he sensed that she was grinding her teeth to stop from ripping off his arm and beating him with it. "Remove your hand."

He did. "Fine. Good luck trying to track him down again."

Ronan straightened his leather jacket, then turned to go back down the alley. He walked maybe ten feet before he could sense her watching him. His spine actually tingled. It was weird. No woman had given him a reaction like that.

He made it to the mouth of the lane and was about to turn left to go back to his car when her voice reached him.

"Wait."

Ivy grimaced at the thought of working with this man, but she was desperate enough to consider it. She'd labored for this tip for months to lose it in a matter of seconds. Who knew how long it would be before she received another reliable one? In the meantime, the demon would kill another woman or two. She didn't know if she could handle that, recognizing she could've done something about it.

She didn't know a lot about cambions. They were rare because it was extremely unusual, if not impossible, to survive a demon attack. It was like being infected with a virus. A fast-acting virus that radically changed your physiology. Thankfully, it could only be passed through blood transfer. According to myth, cambions possessed many of the same powers that demons did. Superstrength, superhealing, super resilience to death. But supposedly it left their humanity intact.

Looking at this man now, she couldn't be sure. It could totally be a trap. He could be working for the demons. It was too bad she didn't have much of a choice.

She walked down the alley to him. "If we work together, it's all my way or the highway."

"Funny considering you have nothing to bargain with, but sure, fine, we'll play it your way."

He had a certain swagger to him, this dark-haired man. It definitely could've been the demon blood infecting him, but she had to admit she kind of liked it. Respected was maybe a better word.

"If I had nothing to bargain with, you wouldn't be so eager to want to team up with me."

He grinned, and she imagined his dark green eyes glinted mischievously. "You got me there."

She eyed him up and down, taking in his solidly built frame and lanky legs. Just by the way he stood, with his arms to his sides, she knew he was well equipped. There was no mistaking the bulge under his jacket, probably a 9mm, or the slight hump under his T-shirt, a bowing knife most likely. He probably had blades strapped to both ankles, as well. At least he came prepared. Maybe it wouldn't be a total waste teaming up with him.

She suspected he was well equipped in the physical department, as well. He made one big target. She could use him as a body shield if worse came to worst.

"What's your name?"

"Ronan Ames."

"Okay, Ronan, we'll try this partnership out. But if I suspect that you are screwing with me or you don't hold up your end of the bargain, I will bleed out that demon blood of yours."

"Deal." He offered his hand.

She took it gingerly, gave a firm shake then released it as quick as she could. It wasn't that she didn't want to shake his hand, it was that touching his skin sent a rush of something pleasant over her flesh. The little hairs on her arms and back of neck were standing at attention. And she wasn't happy about it one bit.

Chapter 3

An hour later, after they had consolidated their individual vehicles—Ronan had stolen his anyway—and amassed their weapons and equipment, Ivy was sitting in the driver's seat of her rusted-out old heavy pickup with a cambion beside her, parked in front of a small bungalow in a part of town usually reserved for the elderly. It definitely was not her idea of an ideal situation. But it was the best option she had right now if she wanted to put down the demon that had been terrorizing the city. If she wanted answers she had to play the game.

"Are you sure this is the place?"

Ronan nodded. "Yeah, I'm sure."

"Where is he, then?"

Even in the dark she could tell that he was staring at her. She could feel the contempt sizzle in the air. "Don't know. I'm not his secretary. I don't have his itinerary loaded on my phone."

"You don't have to be a smart-ass."

"Yeah, I think I do when you ask me dumb-ass questions."

She was about to argue, but knew he had her there. It had been a dumb-ass question. She was just anxious. And anxiety made her on edge, and being on edge made her cranky. It was a vicious cycle.

She was still pissed at him for making her lose the demon in the first place. If he hadn't been so big, and so solid, that he set off her amulet into overdrive, she could've continued the chase down the alley and out onto the street. The demon hadn't had that much of a head start. Sure, he was quick, but so was she.

Ronan smirked. "You would've lost him anyway. He's way too fast even for you."

She glared at him, hoping he could see it even in the dim of the trunk. "You're a mind reader?"

He shrugged. "Don't have to be with you. Your cold stare of death says it all. You're used to blaming others for screw ups."

"You did screw me up," she snarled. "I would've had him if I hadn't run into you."

"Yeah, yeah, keep telling yourself that if it makes you feel better."

"What were you doing in that alley anyway?"

He broke their glaring match and looked out the side window. "None of your business."

"Look, bad blood, I don't like the way—"

He slapped a hand over her mouth. "Shut up for a second."

She was about to rip his hand away when she sensed the same thing he had.

The demon was nearby. She could feel it in the air. Like a horrific dream, like all the happiness in the world had been sucked out of the air. It was a cold clammy feeling on her skin. She shivered in response.

She nodded, and Ronan took his hand away. He pointed to his eyes, then to the house.

Ivy peered through the windshield to the small bungalow. No lights had come on, but she thought she saw movement at one of the darkened windows.

She leaned toward Ronan and whispered, "Is he in the house?"

He nodded without taking his gaze off the house.

"You take the back. I'll go in the front." She

didn't wait for his reply before she quietly opened the door and slid out of the truck. She carefully closed the door but didn't click it shut. Demons possessed superior hearing.

She came around the front just as Ronan got out of the vehicle. They met at the front bumper.

"Don't kill him. I need to talk to him first," she told him.

He just nodded.

Ivy took out her lock-picking kit and headed toward the front door while Ronan crossed the lawn, passed through the side gate and headed around to the back of the house. She stepped up onto the stoop, opened the screen door and tried the knob. It was surprisingly unlocked.

Either the demon had been careless or this was a trap. Ivy went with trap. In her mind, it was always a trap. Nothing was this easy. There was always a catch or two.

She unsheathed one of her silver blades from her back harness, then as quietly as she could, she turned the knob and opened the door. Thankfully the hinges didn't squeak, but she knew it didn't matter. The demon could probably hear her breathing.

It was completely dark inside. She waited a moment just past the threshold for her eyes to adjust. She'd spent plenty of time in darkness so she had better-than-average sight compared to most people. When she could make out the shapes of furniture and other items scattered around the main living room, Ivy stepped forward.

There were no noises in the house. Except for the ticking of a clock nearby and the hum of the furnace, she couldn't discern anything that indicated anyone was at home. But she sensed it. A creepy sensation of foreboding crawled over her skin and she had to suppress the urge to shiver. Someone was here.

As she moved across the room, she had to remind herself that Ronan could also be in the house. Maybe that was who she was sensing. But she had to admit she didn't get a creepy vibe from him. It was another kind of vibe that she didn't want to consider right now.

She moved into the kitchen, and that's when she caught sight of Ronan. He was coming out from the back hall. He lifted his hand in greeting to her. Or to stop her from slicing off a piece of him. She loosened her grip around the hilt of her blade as he came along her side.

"Anything?" he whispered.

She shook her head. "Something's here, though."

"Yeah, I get that, too." He lifted his chin and sniffed the air. "I can smell decomp."

She peered at him curiously.

"There's at least one dead body in this house. One day dead, maybe."

Ivy swung around and searched the shadows of the kitchen. They were either dealing with Sallos's latest kill or his latest creation. She hoped it was the former because if it was the latter, they could be in for a world of hurt.

Revenants were really hard to kill.

They were the undead given life by a demon's black-magic spell. Unlike the zombie lore floating around, these creatures weren't shambling, unintelligent bodies. They possessed speed, tenacity and an irritating lust to kill.

The only way to end them was to cut off their heads and stuff valerian root into their necks. Ivy had a big knife, so that was taken care of, but she didn't have any valerian on her.

"I need to go to the truck."

Even in the dark, she could see Ronan frown. "Are you joking? We're in the middle of something here."

"Watch my back." She moved out of the kitchen before he could protest further. But she could feel him behind her doing as she asked.

She was halfway across the living room when she felt a stir in the stagnant air to her left. She turned that way just as the revenant sprang at her from beside the sofa. What she had erroneously mistaken for three lumpy throw pillows had been a reanimated corpse lying in wait.

It latched onto her left arm with its clawlike fingers and carried her backwards. With its substantial weight behind it—Sallos had killed and resurrected a Goliath—it took them both to the ground. But before it could rip a chunk out of her shoulder with its jagged teeth, Ronan was there kicking it in the head.

The force of Ronan's kick sent it reeling off her and onto its back. Ivy scrambled to her feet but not before the revenant grabbed onto her right leg, trying to dig its fingers into her flesh.

Thank God for the thickness of her jeans, she thought. Never before had she wanted to plant a kiss on Levi Strauss more than she wanted to now.

As she shook her leg to get it off, Ronan shot it in the back. It instantly released her. The blast of his gun echoed around the room.

"That's not going to kill it," she shouted over the ringing in her ears.

"I know, but it got it off you, didn't it?"

She didn't grace him with a response, but turned and prepared for the revenant's next attack. They never stayed down long. It was back up on its feet in a flash and rushing forward.

Ivy unsheathed a second knife and, using defensive holds, she crisscrossed her arms and sliced deep into the revenant's gut. It grunted, stumbled backward, and then looked down as its insides spilled onto the rug. She had to bite down on her lip to stop from retching.

"That'll keep it busy for a few minutes," Ronan offered as he studied the revenant's guts on the ground.

"I need to get the valerian from the truck."

"Go. I've got this covered."

Ivy sidestepped around the confused revenant and rushed out the front door. She ran down the lawn and to the truck. Her bag of herbs and roots was behind the cab seat. She unlocked the truck and rummaged around for her bag. She found it, opened it and grabbed a small plastic bag of the herb. Stuffing it into her pocket, she ran back to the house.

When she walked into the house, the revenant was in a few pieces on the living room rug. One severed arm still moved.

She shook her head. "A little overkill, don't you think?"

Ronan shrugged. "Best to make sure."

She stomped over to the headless torso of the revenant. She opened the plastic bag, took out a pinch of valerian root and shoved it down into the open neck wound. The squishy sensation on her fingers made her head swim and her stomach flop over unpleasantly. She wiped the residual blood and gore onto her pants.

Within a minute, all the squirming pieces of the revenant lay still.

"We should burn the body," Ivy said as she prodded the torso with her boot.

Ronan nodded. "I know a good place to do that."

"Yeah, I bet you do," she muttered under her breath. But she knew he heard her and she didn't care.

"I just saved your ass, lady, so I suggest you be nicer."

She cocked one eyebrow. "Please. I didn't need your help. I would've taken care of it by myself."

"Before or after it had eaten your leg for a midnight snack?"

She smirked. "Whatever. Let's just find a garbage bag, get the pieces together and get this done." She looked around the room. "Obviously, Sallos knew we were coming. He might have other traps for us."

Ronan disappeared into the kitchen and came back with a hefty orange garbage bag. "Found one under the sink." He knelt down and started to fill the bag.

"We should hurry. That shot you took probably woke the neighborhood. Cops will probably be here soon."

She picked up the arm and shoved it into the plastic bag.

"You can't just say thanks, can you?" He stuffed another piece inside. "It's obvious gratitude is beyond your intellectual scope." When the bag was full, Ronan tied it off.

"Can we just move it along?" Ivy didn't want to talk about it. She didn't want to feel gratefulness or anything for this cambion. The less she felt for him, the better.

"Yup, no problem." He hefted the bag over his shoulder. As he walked it swung and hit Ivy in the side of the head. It had enough impact to send her sprawling over the sofa. She had no doubt in her mind that he'd done it on purpose.

Balling her hands into fists, she followed him out of the house, down the front steps and to the truck. After he swung the bag into the back of the truck, she rounded on him. She poked him in the chest with her knuckle.

"Listen to me. I told you this was my way or the highway. So either do what I say or you can get lost. I don't need your running commentary about what I am doing or not doing."

He regarded her with his lips twitching. She

didn't like how he was looking at her. As if she was an amusement to him. "Do you ever relax?"

"No," she sneered. "Relaxing gets people killed."

"You know what else gets people killed? High blood pressure."

Grinding her teeth, she spun on her heel and jumped into the truck. Ronan got in on the other side. She started the truck, put it in gear and drove away from the house.

Under her breath she counted to ten slowly. When she reached ten she looked over at Ronan and asked, "Where are we going?"

"Inner East Bay, down by the harbor."

"Once we do this, then what? What's your next big idea?" She opened her window a crack. She felt like she was suffocating. Ronan's presence was crowding on her. He was a big guy and took up a lot of the space inside the cab. "Sallos knew we were coming. How?"

Ronan rubbed a hand over the stubble on his chin. "I don't know. Maybe because he knew what *you* would do next."

"So this is my fault?"

"He obviously made you the second you walked into that club. You don't exactly fly under the radar, Ivy."

"What about you? Maybe he made you," she

suggested. "Or I know, how about, you're working with him, so he knew we were coming because that was the plan." She thought about his stolen car. Maybe that had been the reason, so it would be easy for him to hook up with her. Except as a hunter she'd stolen plenty of vehicles. It was part of the game.

Cocking his head, he regarded her. "I know there's a brain in that pretty head of yours. So maybe you should use it. What you're proposing is just ridiculous." She hated the mocking tone in his voice.

Without a thought, she yanked the steering wheel to the right and pulled up onto the curb. "Get out."

"What?"

"I said get the hell out of my truck."

"You're being overdramatic, don't you think?"

That was it. She had enough of his lip and they'd been together for only two hours. She balled up her fist and punched him in the side of the face. The force was enough to snap his head back. She had the satisfaction of seeing him bump the other side of his head against the door.

He turned his head back to her, then rubbed at his jaw where she'd clocked him. "Feel better? Got it out of your system? Can we move on now?"

She nodded. "Definitely feel better."

"Good, because we need to keep moving. A cop just pulled up behind us."

Ivy glanced in her rearview mirror. He was right. A police cruiser had just pulled onto the street where they were parked. It would be very bad if he found their big bag of body parts in the truck bed. She suspected that even she wouldn't be able to talk her way out of it.

She put the truck back in gear and pulled out onto the street. The cop car followed her. She kept glancing in the mirror, holding her breath, hoping she didn't see the flashing lights come on.

After they drove another four blocks, the cruiser put on his signal and turned right. Ivy let out the breath she was holding.

Ronan rubbed at his chin again. "You punch pretty hard. Not like a girl at all."

She swiveled in her seat to tell him a thing or two, but the smile on his face had her biting back the words. She couldn't help the grin that lifted her lips.

"Aha, I knew you could smile." His eyes sparkled in amusement. "There's a running rumor out there that it would never happen. That it couldn't."

She shook her head, but she couldn't help the laugh bubbling out of her. "Well, I'm happy to bust that rumor to hell."

"Yeah, I wonder what other rumors we can bust along the way."

Her smile faded then and she turned back to the road. "Keep dreaming."

Although his words bothered her, it was the lusty gleam in his eyes that worried her more. Because truth be told, the butterflies in her stomach had not stopped fluttering since setting her eyes on him in the back alley. And that was always a sign of bad things to come.

Ronan made her body react in ways she hadn't felt for a long time. Lusty thoughts finger walked their way through her mind when she looked at him. He had that dark and dangerous swagger about him that sent her libido into a tizzy. This job was going to be one of the toughest of her career so far. And it had nothing to do with the mark.

Chapter 4

Ronan directed Ivy down to the bay. He knew of a perfect spot to dispose of a body. He'd unfortunately had to use it himself a time or two.

She didn't speak as she parked the truck near the water's edge. She got out and went around back, pulling down the tailgate so they could get at the bag of body parts. Ronan slid out of the truck and then jumped into the back. He thought he surprised her with his agility because she looked at him with those wide blue eyes and a snarl on her lips.

Fog swirled around the tires of the truck. It gave the whole area a creepy vibe. The fact that they were dumping a body just upped that vibe to the nth degree. Moisture settled onto the back of his neck and the backs of his hands. A shiver rushed down his spine as he breathed in the cool night air.

Together they wrestled the bag out of the truck and onto the ground. From there, Ronan dragged it to the bay's shoreline. He opened the bag and began to stuff it with rocks he found around the water's edge. Once Ivy realized what he was trying to accomplish she helped out by finding big boulders to weigh the bag down.

"I see you've done this before," she commented as she dropped a particularly large rock into the bag.

He nodded. "A time or two. Nobody that didn't need killing, though."

"Uh-huh." She barely glanced at him.

He stood back and eyed her curiously. "Is it that you absolutely despise demons in any shape or form, or do you generally loathe everything?"

She didn't give an answer, just took a step back and wiped her dirty hands on her pants.

Ronan tied off the bag and shoved it into the water. It buoyed at the surface for a second or two, then sank down into the inky depths. If it was ever found, it would be quite a ways down the shoreline.

He wiped his hands on his pants, and then looked at Ivy. She was watching the water ripple where the body had gone down. He couldn't read the look on her face, but it wasn't a happy one. Guilt, maybe. Remorse? Interesting considering her hard-assed reputation for slaying demons and the like.

"Now what?" he asked her.

"Regroup, I guess, and try to figure out where Sallos has gone to ground."

"We could go to my place and—"

"Not likely. We'll go to one of my safe houses." She smirked at him. "You'll be blindfolded, of course."

"Well, of course I will." The sarcasm rolled off his tongue.

She ignored it and headed toward the truck. Ronan followed her. "You don't trust much, do you?"

"I trust only one person. And he's unfortunately not around."

Ronan knew she was talking about her brother, Quinn. He'd heard that Quinn had gone to ground a couple of years ago. No one knew where he was or why he was hiding. He wondered if Ivy even knew. And if she didn't, why not?

Maybe this was why she had misgivings about everyone she met. The one person in her life she probably thought she could rely on had left her. Or at least, Ronan could speculate. There were ru-

mors floating around about the Stroms and their
lives and how they'd been born into the hunting
community. He didn't travel in those circles, just
on the fringes, so he heard things now and then.
Which is how he'd known where to find Ivy in
the first place.

Ronan thought it was kind of a lonely way to
go about life. Always looking over your shoulder.
Always wondering who was going to stab you in
the back. Never being able to let down your guard
for one second just in case someone or something
came calling to kick your ass.

He supposed his life wasn't all that different.
He didn't always have to look over his shoulder to
see if someone was sliding a knife into it, but he
did have to be cautious. He survived by procur-
ing things. Usually the hard-to-find type of things.
Items that were not for sale on eBay. Things like
ancient talismans and old lost documents written
in Aramaic. And most of these things he had to
steal. He was good at what he did. He moved like
the shadows and had never been caught. And he
never planned to be.

His career wasn't perfect. Most of his clients
were ruthless and manipulative and shrewd. People he needed to be wary of, or he would be the
one always looking over his shoulder.

She started the truck and they pulled away from

the deserted spot near the water. As she pulled out onto a gravel road, she glanced at him. "There's a blindfold in the glove box. Put it on."

"You're serious?"

"If you don't want to wear it, I can pull over and you can get out right here and now."

He pressed the button on the compartment. It sprang open and he reached in and took out the black cotton blindfold. He ran it through his fingers. "You know the rumors didn't say anything about you being so kinky."

"Did they say anything about me killing you for talking too much?"

"Why, yes, yes they did."

She turned her head to look back at the road, but he caught the little smirk on her lips. Interesting. Maybe she wasn't so indifferent to him after all.

"I'll play your game," he said, wrapping the cloth over his eyes and tying it in back, "but only because I find you quite fascinating."

"I should have brought a gag for your mouth."

"Next time, we can experiment."

He heard her little chuckle and smiled. He then turned his head to the left and listened to the sounds outside the truck—the gravel crunching under the tires, a blast from a ship's horn, the thump of music from one of the dive bars nearby.

He may not be able to see where he was going, but he certainly could hear it. Despite her fears about him, he wasn't about to tell anyone where her safe house was located. He needed her trust. If he was to achieve his grand plan, he needed her more than she would ever know.

An hour later, the truck slowed, turned left up onto a cement pad then eventually came to a soft rolling stop. Ronan heard the telltale drone of a garage door closing. They were in a suburb somewhere to the north. Since pulling away from the bay he'd known what direction they were going and had adjusted his inner compass with every turn she took. It wasn't an exact science, but he felt more secure knowing roughly where he was in the city. Just in case he needed to disappear in a hurry.

Once the door was fully down, his blindfold was yanked from his eyes. He blinked at Ivy and smiled. "Are we there yet?"

She shook her head at him, then opened her door and got out. He did the same. He looked around the garage, noticing the starkness of it. There was no lawn mower parked in the corner, or workbench with tools spread across it. No lawn furniture or boxes of past things stacked in a neat pile along one wall. There was nothing there. No memories, nothing to hold a person to a place.

It suited Ivy to a tee.

"I never pictured you as a suburbanite."

"Which is exactly why this is the perfect cover." She grabbed her bag from the truck and headed for the door to the main house.

As she approached it, a rush of adrenaline kicked in Ronan's gut. He nearly doubled over from the shock of it. Something was off. Something was wrong. He could feel it crawling over his flesh like angry army ants.

Before Ivy could grab the doorknob, he grabbed the back of her jacket and yanked her backwards. He wrapped his arms around her, pinning her arms to her sides.

She struggled against him. "What the hell are you doing?"

"Something's wrong. I can feel it," he said between gritted teeth.

She looked around the garage. "Are you sure? I don't smell anything. No sulfur, no brimstone."

"Sallos has revenants working for him, remember."

"Do you smell decomp, then?"

He shook his head. "It's just a sense of impending doom."

"Let me go and I'll check the door for any signs of disturbance. I put wards on it before I left. I salted it, too."

Instead of letting her go, he picked her up and

carried her back to the truck. He opened the driver's door and shoved her in, following right behind. He grabbed the keys from her hand and stuck them in the ignition.

"What the hell?"

Ronan started the truck and put it in Reverse. He didn't even wait for the garage door to open. He busted through the metal, tearing the door off the frame, and screeched into the street backwards.

"Are you crazy? You just wrecked my place," she shouted, balling her hands into fists, looking like she was going to wail on him.

But she didn't get the chance. By the time he put the truck into Drive, there was the smell of hellfire in the air. It was acrid, like the odor of vinegar.

Ivy must've noticed it, too, because she turned to look out the side window just as a huge fireball erupted from inside her garage.

Chapter 5

Ivy couldn't believe her eyes as Ronan raced down the street away from her soon-to-be destroyed house. Flames were licking the outside of the garage, engulfing it in an orange ball of light.

"Is there anything in the house that's incriminating?"

She shook the daze from her head, and looked at Ronan. "What?"

"In the house? Are there weapons or illegal substances that will lead to your arrest? There're going to be firemen and police all over that place in minutes."

"No. Not in the house. I have a safe buried in the backyard, under the shed."

"We can come back for that later."

She just nodded, then turned around in the seat to face the front and the road ahead of them. Sirens could be heard a few blocks from them. Ivy saw flashing red lights coming from her right about two blocks away.

She remained quiet as they sped away from the scene. She chewed on her finger as the anger built inside. The house was a write-off. She'd spent three months cultivating that safe house. Signing a lease, under a false name of course, moving in, making friendly with the neighbors. Putting up a false wall for others to see. She kept it up so that nothing would seem out of the ordinary. That no red flags went up for the people living next to her. The last thing she needed was nosy people asking about her business.

Now it was all gone. Her cover was blown.

"How did you know?" she asked him without taking her eyes off the road.

"I can sense things. My sixth sense is more advanced than yours."

"Maybe you knew ahead of time." This time she did look at him.

He shook his head. "Jesus, woman. Get your head out of your butt. I am not the bad guy here. I saved your ass."

She sighed, knowing she was just grasping at

straws and lashing out at him because she wanted to destroy something. And he was the closest something, even if he did make the butterflies in her belly stir and the muscles in her thighs clench annoyingly. "I thought I covered my tracks pretty well. I didn't think anyone could find that safe house."

"Sallos isn't just anyone. He's a very powerful demon."

"I know that," she bit out, angry that he would assume she hadn't done her homework on the demon she'd been tracking for months. "But I'm good at what I do. I've been a hunter for almost my whole life. No demon has ever tracked me to my safe house before. No demon has ever gotten the best of me."

"Well, there are first times for everything," Ronan muttered. "You said you never work with a partner, and here I am."

"Yeah, and I regret it every second that ticks by."

This made Ronan chuckle. He rolled down his window. "I think our next step is to find a place to hole up, get cleaned up and figure out how to take this bastard down."

She nodded. Too angry, upset and tired to do anything else. Besides, he was right and it wasn't worth starting an argument over.

About forty minutes later, Ronan parked the truck in front of room 106 at the Lazy Day Motel just outside of San Francisco on the I-880. The place looked old and run-down and the sunny yellow paint didn't do anything to hide that fact. It didn't bother Ivy. She'd stayed in worse places. It was the nature of the business—the life of a hunter constantly on the move.

Ronan had booked them in, gave a false name, paid with cash and unlocked the door for her. Carrying her duffel bag, Ivy shuffled into the room, then tossed her bag onto the big bed. Ronan came in after her, shut the door and bolted it.

He handed her a bottle of water. "I grabbed these from the vending machine in the lobby."

She took it, uncapped it and took a swallow. "Thanks." She set the bottle down on the worn and scarred table and looked around the room, trying to avoid looking at the bed too long. She had no intention of using it for anything other than sleeping and Ronan wasn't going to be joining her.

"Why do they insist on decorating these places in puke yellows and greens?"

"Must think it's soothing."

"It just makes me want to blow my brains out with my shotgun."

Ronan laughed. "They should put that in one of their brochures. 'Come to the Lazy Day Motel, the perfect place to put up your feet and blow your brains out.'"

A smile tugged at her lips, but she hid it by walking into the adjoining bathroom. It was one of the smallest bathrooms she'd ever been in. There was a small sink, a cracked mirror above it, a small toilet and a narrow box masquerading as a shower. But at least there was running water. She hoped it was hot, but at this point any temperature would do.

She peered out of the bathroom. Ronan was busy sitting on the bed, counting the rounds in his 9mm clip. "I'm going to shower." He just nodded to her and continued to count his bullets.

She shut the door. Or attempted to. The hinges weren't straight, so the door didn't close properly. And because she couldn't close it properly, she couldn't lock it. She hoped the cambion valued his life and wouldn't dare come into the bathroom while she was in the shower.

Ivy quickly shed her clothes and unstrapped all her knife harnesses. The one on her back, the two along her sides and the two around her ankles. She felt ten pounds lighter. She then stepped into the plastic box and yanked the curtain down the rod, but noticed there were two huge holes in the sheet. Sighing heavily, she twisted the water valve and hoped for the best.

Thankfully, wonderful scalding-hot water sprayed from the shower nozzle. She tilted her face up to it and let it cascade over her, washing away the night's dirt, gore and disappointment. She didn't have any soap, so she did her best at scrubbing her body and hair with her hands.

As she ran her hands down the length of her hair, she heard a rap at the busted door. Her first instinct was to cover herself, but she was too damn tired and she couldn't be bothered, so when the door opened she just stood there defiantly. A cool breeze brushed over her backside. She glanced over her shoulder and through one of the holes. Ronan stood in the doorway, his hand still on the doorknob, his eyes glued to the rips in the shower curtain.

"Is there something you want?" she asked, although that may have not been the best question considering the situation. Or considering the dark look in his eyes.

But it was enough to raise his gaze a little and for him to speak. "I'm running across the street to the burger joint. I just wanted to know if you were hungry."

"Whatever. Just get out of this bathroom."

He backed out of the room and swung the door shut, but it popped open again.

Ivy ignored it and finished her shower. She

twisted the taps closed and grabbed the semi-clean towel hanging on the rack. She sniffed it. It at least smelled like bleach and nothing else offensive.

Stepping out of the plastic box, she patted herself dry then redressed in her old clothing. She kept the harnesses off for now. At least her skin was fairly clean, though she'd have to live with the funky stench coming from her shirt. Revenant was difficult to get out of cotton.

Feeling a little bit more human, she came out of the bathroom and went to her bag. She unzipped it and grabbed her cell phone. She had some calls to make to find out what happened. How did Sallos find her house? Or maybe it wasn't even Sallos, but she didn't believe in coincidences, so he had to be the demon who had rigged her house to blow with demon fire.

She punched in the number for an old hunting buddy named Jake. He was usually pretty reliable with information. He had a few scumbag informants that hung around demons and the like. He answered on the third ring.

"Ivy, baby, what's shaking?"

"Your head will be if you call me baby again." She sat down on the bed, realizing how tired she was.

He chuckled. "What's up? You need something?"

"Has there been any word out there on me? Someone really interested in where I'm at?"

"Someone's always interested in where you are at, Ivy." He paused. "Did something happen?"

"One of my safe houses was compromised."

"Shit." He drew the word out. "That's harsh."

"Yeah, my thoughts exactly."

"If someone's been asking questions about you, it hasn't been to me."

She nodded. Jake was a stand-up guy. She knew he wouldn't blab any info about her to anyone. He'd hunted with her brother and even with her dad before he'd died five years ago. "Okay, thanks, Jake."

"Anything else, my one and only love?"

She laughed. "Yeah, if you get wind about a demon named Sallos, let me know right away."

"You got it." He disconnected.

Ivy flipped her phone closed then tossed it back into her bag. She had other calls to make but her stomach was grumbling and she was looking forward to Ronan returning with some food.

She lay back on the bed and stared up at the ceiling. Her opinion of Ronan was starting to change. But only a little. He'd saved her ass, so she granted him a reprieve from thinking of him as a darkness-sucking demon. And he was getting her some food. That always counted for something.

As if to punctuate her rumbling belly, the room door opened and Ronan walked in with two bags of food. "I hope you're hungry. I didn't know what you liked, so I got you pretty much one of everything." He crossed the room and handed her a white paper bag.

"Thanks." She opened the bag and inhaled the delectable smells. "Jesus, that smells amazing." She reached in and pulled out a double burger, loaded. She unwrapped it and took a healthy bite. The spiced greasy flavor exploded in her mouth and she closed her eyes in delight and sighed. She finished it in another three bites. As she chewed the last of it, she reached into the bag for more. She pulled out a large order of fries.

"There's no ketchup."

Ronan tossed her a couple of packets. She caught them, ripped them open and squeezed the ketchup all over her fries.

"I've never seen a woman eat like you do."

"Yeah, well, I doubt you've met any women like me."

He smiled around his food. "That's for sure."

"I'm not sure if that was a compliment or an insult." She shoved three fries into her mouth. She had to admit that she enjoyed their banter. It had been a while since she'd met a man that could dish it out and take it in equal measure.

"What would make you share those fries?"

She laughed out loud. A full guffaw. It felt good to let it out, to let go. She offered him the box. "Either remark will get you half the box."

"Then it was a compliment."

Ronan reached over and grabbed a handful, and set them onto his spread-out burger wrapper on the table. Happily, he dipped them into a torn-open ketchup pack and ate them with gusto.

She watched for a bit, wondering what his motives really were. Yes, he said he was after the same demon. For the first time, she wanted to know why. And why partner with her? Sure, she was the best, but given her reputation he must've known that she was impossible to work with.

Why would a man subject himself to her belligerent ways if he could've gotten information from another source?

He was obviously a glutton for punishment.

"So," he said after chewing, "did you find out anything?"

"I talked to a source and he hasn't caught wind of anyone asking around about me. But that doesn't necessarily mean much. He's not the only hunter out there. Though he is the only one that I can tolerate."

"Anyone else you can contact?"

"Maybe." She finished her fries and dumped the

box into the white paper bag. "What about you? You must have contacts."

He looked at her for a second, then wiped his fingers on the paper napkin. "I do, but you're not going to like them."

Demons. She should've known.

She got up, pitched the bag into the garbage bin, and then stretched out onto the bed. "No, I probably won't."

Ronan checked his watch. "It's two now. I can't talk to my contact until three. So catch some sleep while you can."

Ivy smooshed up the pillow behind her head and closed her eyes. "I plan to."

As she tried to relax her mind, she felt a dip on the mattress next to her. Slowly she opened her eyes and looked to her right. Ronan was fluffing his own pillow behind his head.

"Excuse me?"

He snorted at her. "Please. You can relax. You're definitely not my type."

"Oh, you probably like them with black irises and sulfur for blood."

"Nah." He rolled over onto his side, giving her his back. "I like women with souls."

She flinched as if struck. The harshness of his statement threw her for a loop. She supposed she'd been treating him badly but she was sure she didn't deserve such a scathing remark. Did she?

Ivy didn't dignify his statement with a response, and she turned onto her side, as well. She punched the pillow under her head and closed her eyes again. She wouldn't let him get to her. But after ten minutes of lying there listening to his rhythmic breathing, she realized he was already getting to her in more ways than one.

Chapter 6

Ronan slept for about forty minutes. He had the ability to nod off quickly, go under for a deep sleep and wake up fresh and alert. He didn't sleep much as it was. He attributed that to the demon blood running through him. Full-blooded demons never slept. Gave them more time to cause chaos and havoc on the world.

He moved carefully off the bed so as to not rouse Ivy. When he was up he looked down at her. She slept like she did everything else—with fierce conviction. Her forehead was wrinkled in concentration and it looked like she was grinding her teeth. Both hands were curled into fists.

It looked like she'd bolt up at any moment and punch him in the gut.

But despite all that, she was riveting. She had the quality that made men stand to attention. Made men want to stare into those fierce blue eyes for an eternity, to wait, to hope that she would press those amazing full lips to theirs.

Not that Ronan was thinking of kissing her. It was just she possessed a mouth made to be kissed. It was hard to imagine wasting that tasty pout.

Grabbing his gun and both his knives, he crept out of the room and went around to the back of the motel to the barren, abandoned field that was there. It was a perfect setup for what he needed to do next.

He cleared a spot about six feet in diameter in the soil. After finding a decent stick, he drew a pentagram in the circle of dirt. Then he inscribed the symbol for one particular demon he knew. Daeva. She was a lust demon. Lust demons were more apt to make deals than the other denizens of hell.

Once that was done, he needed to activate the "call." Taking out one of his blades, he cupped it in his palm and drew the blade across his skin. The immediate sharp sting of the steel made him suck in a breath. Holding his hand up over the sigil, blood ran down his hand and dripped onto the dirt. The black spots immediately soaked into the ground.

It wouldn't be long before the call was answered. Daeva was usually quite prompt.

Ronan pulled out a thin piece of gauze from his pocket. He always came prepared. He wrapped it around his palm, stemming the flow of blood. Just as he finished tying it off, an audible pop sounded before him. The smell of brimstone and some exotic spices filled the air. He looked up to face the demon.

She smiled. "Well, hello, Ronan. What can I do you for?"

Ronan shook his head at her play on words. It was an old joke.

"Get it? What can I *do* you for?" She laughed; the sound was like tinkling bells.

"Yeah, I get it, Daeva. It just isn't funny."

She took a step toward him, mindful of the lines of the pentagram that she was bound inside. "So, honey, what can I really do for you?"

Out of all the demons he'd run across, Daeva was the only one he liked. She was fun and funny and sexy as all get out with her long crimson hair and startling gray eyes. And she really didn't follow the usual demon code. She didn't look for ways to get out of the pentagram and rip your innards out. As long as he'd been doing business with her, he'd yet to see her do any real harm to anyone. She just liked to seduce people. And he really didn't see the harm in that.

"I need information."

"About?"

"Sallos."

"I see." She tapped one long fingernail against her cherry-stained lips. "I heard he was being a really bad boy."

"Yes, he's murdering women. Lots of them. He needs to be stopped."

"Oh, I agree, Ronan, no doubt about that. But what will you give me in return for my information?"

"What do you want?" He knew it was a mistake to ask an open-ended question to a demon, but he trusted Daeva. Sort of.

"I want to meet her."

"Who?"

"Who do you think? Ivy Strom, of course."

"Why?"

She pursed her lips, then fluffed her hair. "I have my reasons."

"And those would be?" The voice that came was as frigid as the Arctic winds. Ronan whirled around to see Ivy walking out of the shadows to stand beside him.

"None of your business, really." Daeva smiled at the unexpected arrival.

Ivy bristled a little, and Ronan sensed she was about to do something stupid, but at the last second she seemed to settle down and sighed instead. "Well, we've met, so now you can tell us about Sallos."

"We haven't been properly introduced." Daeva looked at Ronan. "Will you do the honors?"

He sighed and shook his head. He had a bad feeling that he was going to pay for this in some way. Either from Daeva or from Ivy. There seemed to be some rivalry between them that he couldn't figure out. "Daeva, Seductress of Shadows, this is Ivy Strom…"

"Hunter of all Demons," Ivy finished for him.

Daeva chuckled, then offered her hand. "It's a pleasure to meet you, Ivy Strom. I've heard so much about you."

Ivy looked at the offered hand, then to Ronan. He shrugged. He had no clue what Daeva was up to. He'd never seen her behave this way.

"From who?"

"The word gets around. Hell's not that big, you know. When one of us comes back, sent back by you, you can bet he's right pissed about it."

Ivy took a step forward so the edge of her boot

touched the line of the pentagram. She reached through the binding and grasped Daeva's hand.

From the look of rapt fascination on the demon's face, Ronan almost expected her to pull Ivy into the pentagram. He reached over and grabbed Ivy around the waist.

The two women shook hands, and then Ivy pulled back and whipped around to glare at him. "What the hell are you doing?"

He released his hold on her, then sheepishly took a distancing step away. "Nothing." He looked at Daeva; she was giving him a similar look.

He found the whole thing strange. It was like some weird female bonding thing that he just didn't get. Next thing he knew, they would be going out shoe shopping or something.

He cleared his throat of the awkwardness he felt. "Okay, now that that's done, tell us where Sallos is located."

Daeva cocked her hip and wrapped a finger in her hair, playing with it both innocently and seductively. "Give me a piece of paper and I can give you an address."

Ronan opened his duffel bag and came away with a notebook. He tore off a piece of paper and handed it to her. The demon took it, then ran her index finger over it. "There." She handed it back to Ronan.

He looked down at it. There was an address scrolled on the paper in bright red. He didn't even want to consider what she'd used for ink.

Ivy took it from him. She glanced at it, then at Daeva. "This better be right."

"Oh, it is, honey. Don't you worry your pretty little head."

By the look of fury on Ivy's face, Ronan decided it would probably be best if he ended the "call" and sent Daeva back to wherever she came from. "Thank you, Daeva, for the information."

"My pleasure, Ronan, darling. I always love it when you come a-knocking at my door." Then she put her gaze on Ivy. "It was a pure pleasure meeting you, Ivy Strom. Say hi to your brother for me, will you?" She smiled, blew her a kiss and then snapped her fingers. She was gone in a flash and a puff of spices.

"What was that about?" Ronan asked.

Ivy shrugged. "I have no idea. Quinn's exorcised a lot of demons, so maybe she's got a bone to pick with him." Ivy folded the piece of paper and shoved it into her pants pocket. "Nice choice of contact, by the way."

He gathered his gear back up and put it in his bag. "She's always reliable."

"What does she usually ask for, for payment?"

He picked up the bag and swung it over his

shoulder. He grinned. "Wouldn't you like to know?" With a bit of a swagger in his step, Ronan walked past Ivy to return to the hotel.

He felt her piercing gaze on his back all the way to their hotel room. It made him grin like a fool who'd just won a bet. He was getting to her, just like he'd planned.

Chapter 7

When they got back to the room, Ivy sat down on the edge of the bed and unfolded the paper that the demon had given them. Her hands shook a little, and she put them down at her sides so Ronan wouldn't see them. She was a bit unnerved by the exchange between her and Daeva. When she'd shaken her hand, she got the overwhelming sense that the demoness didn't mean her any harm and, in fact, had been pleased to meet her. It had been strange, to say the least.

"Fifty-five Fourth Street."

"That's what it says."

"That's downtown. Do you have a map?"

"Better." Ronan reached into his pack and pulled out his iPhone.

She shook her head in disbelief.

"What? Don't you have one? I can get all kinds of info on here. Maps and internet, voice dialing, even Facebook." He grinned at that last one.

"Just look up the address, please."

He tapped the screen what seemed like a hundred times. His face paled after a few minutes. He looked up at Ivy. "We might have a problem."

"What?"

He handed her the phone. She looked down at the information displayed on the screen. She sighed. "You have got to be kidding. Is she serious with this info?"

Ronan leaned back in the worn chair at the table. "She's never given me bad information before. I trust it."

"It's the Marriott Marquis, Ronan. How are we supposed to get in there and trap a demon without injuring thousands of people?"

"Carefully?"

"Not to mention having the cops involved. If we start a scene, and you know there will be one, they'll be called in for sure."

"I don't know, but this is good intel. We can't let it go to waste. We might not get another chance at this one."

She sighed, then ran a hand over her face. He was right. They may never get another chance to find Sallos. She'd worked months to get the one tip on him for the club. The odds were if they didn't act now, Sallos would kill again, maybe more than once, before she could catch him.

"Do you have a plan?" she asked Ronan between clenched teeth. She hated deferring to someone else for answers. She was used to relying on herself to have a good plan of action.

"The most logical thing to do is to check in and snoop around."

"There are over a thousand rooms in the hotel. Even if we both dressed up as cleaning staff we'd never be able to search all those rooms."

"We won't have to. Sallos is all about the chase. He'll be out and about on the prowl. There are a few bars in the hotel. He'll be staking out one, if not more, for his next victim."

She nodded, then handed the phone back to him. "You're right." She ran her hands over her pants, then stood. She glanced at her watch. "It's four a.m. We can't check in until what? Three in the afternoon?"

"Four."

"That gives us some time to prepare."

Ronan nodded. "Yeah, and find something else

to wear. We can't go into a posh hotel like the Marriott wearing stained denim and leather."

"My place is likely destroyed, plus I imagine it'll still be swarming with police."

"Then I suggest shopping." He reached into his back pocket and pulled out four credit cards. He tossed them onto the bed.

Ivy reached down and plucked one. She read it. "Alex Irvine?"

He nodded. "Yup. I'm also Peter Jacobs, Brian Frost and my personal favorite, Harry Ennis."

She groaned, but couldn't stop her lips from twitching upwards. "If you tell me that the middle initial is P, I'm going to smack you really hard."

"Nah, I didn't go that far." He laughed. "But they each have about a five grand limit, so I'm sure we can buy you something hot to wear."

She glared at him. "I will not be wearing something hot, thank you very much."

"Why not? You could definitely pull it off."

She didn't like that gleam in his eye again. It was the second time she'd seen it in the past few hours. The first time had been in the bathroom when he came across her showering. The cambion had another think coming if he thought there was going to be anything sexual between them.

They were working together. Work and sex didn't mix.

And why was she even thinking about that anyway? It was more than just a work thing. It was a demon blood thing. Just because the man was devastatingly good-looking with wide, powerful shoulders and a smile that could disarm a nuclear weapon didn't mean she was in any way thinking about having sex with him.

She cocked her hip and pinned him with a look she hoped came across angry and not sexually frustrated. "Do I seriously have to go over the rules of our limited partnership again?"

"No." He shook his head. "Just messing with you, boss. I know that there couldn't possibly be a sexual being under all that steel and ice."

She gaped at him. But he never gave her a chance to respond before he was bouncing on the bed, stuffing the pillow behind his head and closing his eyes.

"Since we have some time to kill, I'm going to catch a few more hours of sleep."

She glared down at him, but he was impervious to it. After another minute, he was snoring soundly.

Angry, she stared at him some more, willing him to wake up and fight with her. That way, maybe she wouldn't be so aware of the muscle tick at his strong jawline and the urge she had to trace a fingertip over it to smooth it away.

She turned around on her heel and paced the room. She'd gone too long without a man in her life. Her libido was flaring up like a bad rash. She thought it ridiculous that just having this man stretched out on the bed in front of her, his long legs spread a little, with his deep breathing and his tantalizing male scent in her nostrils was enough to have her heart racing and her gut swirling.

Clenching her hand into a fist, she rubbed it down her leg. She had to get it together. There was no time for distractions. Especially tall, dark and extremely dangerous ones like Ronan. If she wanted to catch Sallos and send him back to hell she had to concentrate on doing just that. And not on fantasizing about the cambion in the bed in front of her.

She also needed more sleep. She was running on barely three hours and had to get some more if she was to be fully functional later when they would have to battle a Great Duke of Hell.

She turned and looked at the bed again. Ronan had the right idea. It irked her that he could turn it off just like that though. Close his eyes and be out instantaneously. Ivy's brain just didn't work like that. She was constantly thinking, constantly worrying. Constantly on the lookout for the next big thing to sneak up behind her and bite her on her ass.

She sat down on the bed, then lay back. She had to shove Ronan over a bit so she could fit comfortably. Her elbow did nothing to move him. Then he just mumbled and turned over onto his side. It made enough room for her to sleep.

She tucked a hand behind her head and closed her eyes. She willed herself to sleep. And not to think about two hundred pounds of pure masculinity lying next to her and how it would feel if he rolled right on over top of her and pinned her to the mattress with the sure power of his massive frame.

She imagined he would nudge her legs apart with his knee and settle in between her thighs. She would feel the hard length of him nestled against her groin. She'd be eager for him, open for him, wet for him....

Cursing, she sat up, got off the bed and went to sit in the chair. She slid down and put her feet up on the table. She'd slept in worse places.

Ronan opened his eyes. He stared at the hotel wall. He didn't dare turn around to see if Ivy was sleeping or not. It had taken all he had not to grin when she'd glared down at him earlier. He'd faked falling asleep. He was sure his snores sounded authentic. But he'd been wide-awake the whole time. Awake and aware.

Especially when she'd plopped down beside him on the bed. He'd been vividly aware of her then.

Her scent had tickled his senses. His gut had clenched, as had his hands. They'd wanted to reach over and touch her. Especially now that he'd seen her in the shower. After seeing parts of her incredible body through the tears in the shower curtain, he could think of nothing else but touching her. To see if she was as strong and hard as she looked. If her soft parts were as silky as he imagined they would be.

He wanted to see if she would yield under his caresses or fight him all the way. Either one would've been fine with him. Just as long as he could have her hard and fast.

He'd been warned that she was difficult to work with, impossible to deal with and a massive pain in the ass. He'd experienced all that firsthand. Despite all of that, though, he wanted her. He wanted to melt that icy exterior of hers. To prove that there was an actual feeling woman underneath all that prickly armor and attitude.

He loved a challenge. He'd been dealt one right after another his whole life. He'd survived being infected with demon blood. He could survive and would even flourish under the reign of one Ivy Strom.

So he closed his eyes once more and calmed his mind. He'd need another good five hours of sleep before he could even fathom dealing with her again.

Chapter 8

After rushing around town shopping and doing damage control on Ivy's safe house—it had been burned down to the ground and they couldn't get to the safe in the backyard—Ronan and Ivy checked into the San Francisco Marriott Marquis.

The pretty hotel clerk handed Ronan back his credit card. "Thank you, Mr. Ennis, we have you checked into one of our executive suites for one night."

Ivy rolled her eyes at him as he grinned at the clerk. "Thank you, Holly."

"My pleasure." Holly batted her eyes at him. "Do you need help with your bags?"

"No, thank you. My wife likes to handle that."

Leaning on the counter, he smiled at Ivy. "Don't you, darling?"

It took all she had not to bop Ronan in the mouth. Instead she gave him a tight smile and rolled both bags. Without waiting for him, she started for the bank of elevators.

She couldn't believe she let him talk her into posing as a couple, but it made sense and would help them keep a low profile until they found Sallos and trapped him so they could interrogate him. She'd even agreed to tone down her usual harsh exterior.

When they went shopping she bought a pant-suit in cream and three-inch heels in gold. She was wearing the outfit now and it wasn't as uncomfortable as she'd first thought it would be. The silky material of the trousers actually felt nice on her skin, luxurious even. And the heels, well she kind of liked them. Made her legs feel more powerful. They did amazing things to her calf muscles. She also bought a cocktail dress for later at Ronan's encouraging. They were going to be going up to The View Lounge tonight on reconnaissance.

Ronan caught up to her at the elevators just as one chimed and its doors opened. Some people streamed out, and Ivy and Ronan went in alone. Ronan pressed the button for the fifteenth floor.

"Do you really have to flirt with every woman

we come across?" She'd meant to joke with him, but even she could hear the slight bitterness in her voice. She coughed into her hand afterward to cover it, but by the glint in Ronan's eye he'd heard it loud and clear.

"Are you jealous?"

She snorted. "Not likely. It's just bothersome, especially since we should be playing it under the wire. Do we really want people to notice us?"

"It never hurts to be charming to people. When the shit hits the fan and bad stuff happens, do you really think that pretty young thing at the counter is going to tell the cops about the seductively attractive man she flirted with at the counter? Or would she be more inclined to mention the quiet shifty-eyed steely couple that checked in mere hours before everything went down?"

She folded her arms across her chest. "Just because I can see your point doesn't mean you are right."

"Yeah, it does."

The doors opened; Ronan grabbed his bag and walked out. Ivy followed him. They walked in silence down to their room. Thankfully, they didn't run into anyone who would force them to play the happy married couple.

Ronan slid the key card into the lock, the little green light blinked on and he opened the door for her. She went in, pulling her black compact luggage behind her.

The room was big and elegant. It looked like how she would have imagined an executive suite. Clean, angled, everything in its place, with gold pillows on the modest sofa and a dark wooden desk along one wall. But it was a really nice room and she smiled.

It wasn't every day that she got to stay in a decent hotel. Most of the time, she stayed in rundown dirt-bag motels along long lonely highways. So although she was on the job and had to work with Ronan, she was going to enjoy this small luxury just for a little while.

She nodded at Ronan. "Nice room."

He rolled his luggage into the open bedroom area, setting it beside the king-size bed. He sat on the edge and bounced on the mattress. "Nice and firm." He gave her a wide cheesy grin.

"You're sleeping on this here sofa."

"The hell I am." He stood and walked over to her. "We'll flip for the bed." He dug into his pants pocket and came away with a quarter. "Heads I get the bed, tails you do." He flipped it off his thumb, caught it in his palm and slapped it on the back of his other hand. He showed the coin.

It was heads.

"I win."

She shook her head. "I didn't agree to play." Giving him her back, she wandered into the huge bathroom. There was a jetted tub. She smiled and ran a finger along the porcelain. God, she'd love a long hot soak in the tub.

"We should probably go over the plan," Ronan said from the other room.

With a heavy sigh, Ivy returned to the living room and sat on the sofa. "Where do you want to start?"

After an hour, they had hammered out a reasonable strategy. It was a decent one considering their circumstances. Ronan had smarts. She liked how he thought. He was almost as diabolical as she was. Almost.

Afterwards, she changed clothes into something unassuming—jeans, T-shirt, runners and a ball cap—and told Ronan she was going to get a lay of the hotel and figure out their exit strategy if everything went wrong. Which, considering the circumstances, was an acute possibility.

She scoped out the lobby and the main restaurant. She also took an elevator ride up to the thirty-ninth floor to check out The View Lounge. There weren't too many people at the bar or at the tables near the floor-to-ceiling windows. But she suspected that would change in a few hours.

The concierge in the lobby told her it was usually packed by ten.

She did a quick scan of the place, took in the security detail at the door, where the main bar was situated, where the exit was and how the long the bank of windows stretched along the lounge. Even from where she stood, the view of the city below was spectacular. She looked over the particular clientele already seated and drinking and knew that Sallos wouldn't be able to resist the temptation of finding his next victim here. Most of his past victims had been young women known to drink and party, so hitting an upscale place like this with older, wealthier women would be something the demon would just have to sample.

Once she was satisfied with her reconnaissance, Ivy returned to the hotel room. When she entered, Ronan was sitting on the sofa, sharpening one of his many blades. The scene brought back memories of hunting with her brother Quinn and all the times they'd shared this together. The prehunting stage. Gearing up for the big one. A time they both knew could be their last.

Pushing thoughts of her brother from her mind, she came in, took off her cap, tossed it on the table and ran a hand through her hair. "There are two exits from the lounge. One to the elevators and another to the stairwell. And there appears to be one security guard near the front entrance."

"We could position weapons at various points on different floors," he replied. "In the event of trouble, we can subdue the guard, then take the stairs. You exit out on the thirtieth floor and I could come out on the twentieth. We rendezvous down at street level by the truck."

She nodded. "Sounds good. Smart."

"Yeah, who knew I was good-looking *and* intelligent?"

She shook her head but ended up smiling. He had an infectious way about him. He was either making her angry or making her laugh. Both stirred up unwanted feelings.

There was a knock on the door.

Ivy swung around toward it, hands up, ready to fight.

Ronan stood. "I ordered room service. I thought we both could eat something substantial." He opened the door. The attendant wheeled in a tray of steaming hot food. He nodded to Ivy and Ronan, then left after Ronan tipped him ten bucks.

Ivy lifted up the lids on the plates. The incredible smell of steak and potatoes wafted to her nose. She smiled.

"After watching you scarf down that burger and

fries the other night, I thought maybe you could use a nice thick juicy steak."

"You thought right." She reached down and plucked a piece of steamed broccoli from the plate.

"I also drew you a bath." He took the lid off the other plate and leaned down to inhale the rich delectable smells.

"You did what?"

"Drew you a bath. I found some bath salts, as well. I put them in." He shrugged. "Smells good."

She pushed open the bathroom door and walked in. The scent of vanilla came to her nose on a puff of steam and she smiled. She glanced over her shoulder at Ronan, who was watching her.

"The water's still hot."

He wriggled his fingers. "One of the many tricks I inherited with the demon blood."

"Oh." She cleared her throat. It was suddenly feeling dry from emotions that had no business showing up. "Why did you do this?"

"I thought you needed it. Thought you'd like it."

She studied him for a few more seconds then said, "Thanks." She nodded to the food tray. "Don't eat my steak."

"I won't." His lips lifted into a smile.

She went into the bathroom, closed the door and leaned against it. The cambion was turning out to be far more complicated than she'd first thought, and she was sure that was going to become a huge problem in the future.

She stripped off her clothes, and with a contented sigh she slipped down into the deep-jetted tub. The water was still deliciously hot and silky from the bath salts, it slicked her skin. Twisting a knob she kicked in the jets, then rested her head on the back of the tub and closed her eyes.

She couldn't remember the last time she had indulged like this, maybe never. Growing up had been tough and meager as she'd moved around with her dad and brother, chasing monsters around the country. She'd never had a manicure or a pedicure. She knew how to dress like a lady and act like one, something she'd learned from magazines and TV, but she'd never ever felt like one. Until this very second.

She wondered how Ronan knew this had been what she'd needed and wanted. Sometimes she questioned whether he could read her mind. Maybe the demon blood in his veins gave him certain abilities. Reading her might very well be one. God, she hoped not. It could get embarrassing for her if he could.

Or it could've been the man inside him. An instinct that drove a man to want to pamper a woman, to shield her, to protect her, to love her....

Her eyes flashed open at that. Licking her lips,

she realized how tight her throat was. She sighed, then laid her head back again. She had better keep her thoughts straight. On the plan. On the mission. And not on the man with the hard face and soft heart sitting on the sofa in the other room.

Chapter 9

For the next hour and a half, Ronan ate, finished sharpening his knives, reloaded his gun and paced the room trying not to think of Ivy naked and wet and soapy in the bathtub.

A half hour ago, she'd slipped out of the bathroom wrapped in one of the complimentary terrycloth white robes, grabbed some food, ate it then took her bag and went back in.

Then he started thinking about her getting dressed after lathering her skin with moisturizers and body lotions. The thought had actually made him start to sweat.

So instead he busied himself getting dressed for the big event. They were going in chic casual, so as not to stick out like sore thumbs. But he had a feeling Ivy was going to stick out anyway. And not as a sore thumb, but as an enchantress. Even in a T-shirt and a pair of jeans, she was dangerously beautiful. He couldn't imagine what it would do to him to see her in the little black number he knew she'd bought for tonight.

He took a sip of the scotch he'd poured earlier and paced the room some more waiting for her to emerge. Finally, the bathroom door opened.

And he nearly dropped his glass.

The silky black material, what little there was, clung to her generous curves as she walked into the room. Her pale skin glowed like moonlight in contrast with the dark dress. She was wearing a short blond wig, which showcased the long sweep of her elegant neck. There was a spot just below her ear that he had a sudden urge to trail his tongue up and down.

He swallowed the saliva pooling in his mouth and said, "Um, wow, Ivy, you look, um…"

His stammering made her smile, and pink stained her cheeks. She was blushing, just a little. "Thank you."

"You look amazing," he said, after finally collecting his senses.

Her gaze studied him, as well. "So do you, actually."

Ronan ran a hand down his shirt. He'd settled on simple dark wool trousers and a button-up dress shirt in a shade of navy. "Thanks. Feels weird without my leather, though."

She laughed. "I know what you mean."

He ran his gaze over her from head to toe, taking every glorious inch of her in. Then he paused. "Ah, where are your blades?"

She lifted one brow. "Wouldn't you like to know?"

"Yes, actually I would."

"Well, you're not getting a peep show, so just forget about it." She picked up her clutch purse from the table. He knew inside she had holy water, blessed chalk, angelica, a silver cross that pulled out into a dagger and some premade devil's-trap stickers. You just peeled off the back and stuck it onto a chair, or the floor, or anywhere you wanted the demon to be held. He'd heard about Ivy's invention and it was pretty cool.

As satisfied as he was going to get, he offered his arm to her. "Shall we?"

With a little shake of her head and a twitch of her lips, she took his arm and they left the room in search of their target.

The View Lounge was busy when they stepped off the elevator and entered. Most of the orange and yellow chairs were occupied. There were a few people standing together in various groups, talking and laughing. A lot of eyes turned toward them as they approached the bar. Ronan figured it was all because of Ivy. Except there were a few pairs of female eyes sizing him up.

They went to the bar, thankfully found two vacant stools and ordered. Ivy ordered a raspberry martini and he had a scotch on the rocks. Once they had their respective drinks, they surveyed the bar for Sallos.

The plan was for Ivy to lure the demon away from the crowd, preferably near the elevators and stairwell exit. Ronan would slap a devil's trap on him and they could carry him out, down the stairs to a remote place to question him and ultimately end him. But Ronan knew that even the best-laid plans could go to shit.

It didn't take long to find him. The demon was predictable, at best. Ronan spotted a pair of older women sitting at a table near the immense window, and Sallos was holding court. Both women looked completely enthralled with him, hanging on to every word he spoke.

"Found him."

Ivy leaned into him, as if to whisper something private. "Where?"

"Ten o'clock."

With her drink to her mouth, she swirled in her

seat and checked it out. "He seems pretty comfortable."

"Yeah, both ladies look hooked. Do you think he'd take both?"

"I wouldn't put it past the bastard. He's in show-off mode now that he thinks he's escaped us twice."

"Maybe we should wait until he makes his move out of here. By the way those two are looking at him, and their body language, I would say that will be very soon."

"When they go, you slap him with the trap and I'll make sure the women are removed from the situation."

"Now, be nice."

She smiled and it was sexy and wicked and made his stomach clench. "I'm always nice."

"No, you're not," he said, but he smiled in return.

For the next thirty minutes, Ronan and Ivy drank their drinks and watched Sallos as he seduced the two women. It wasn't long before the three of them stood, giving each other those knowing looks. The looks that said they had made the decision to leave together and finish their evening in privacy.

Ronan and Ivy waited as the trio passed them to head toward the bank of elevators. They set their empty drink glasses on the bar, then slid off the bar stools. Ivy slipped him one of her devil's-trap stickers, then started for the elevators.

Tucking the decal in the palm of his right hand, Ronan wrapped his other hand around Ivy's waist. She didn't protest when he pulled her closer. They needed to keep up the pretense as a happy couple just until they reached the elevators. Also, he liked having her close. Her scent, mixed with the vanilla she'd bathed in, wafted to his nose and he inhaled it deep.

As they neared the little elevator lobby, Ronan sensed something was wrong. He paused and pulled Ivy tighter to him.

She frowned at him. "What are you doing?"

"Something's off."

Before Ivy could respond, the two older women came flying out from the enclave, teeth bared, fingers twisted into claws. They shrieked like banshees as they attacked Ronan and Ivy.

Ronan blocked his face from nails tearing him apart. He pushed one woman away but she came back, just as fierce, eyes wild, foaming at the mouth. Ivy was having just as much trouble with the brunette attacking her.

"What the hell?" She grabbed the woman's wrist. "Why are they attacking us?"

"They're enchanted. Powerful demons can

sway people to do their bidding without a spell or possession." Ronan shoved the woman spitting and clawing at him into the wall.

"How come I've never heard of that?" Ivy had the brunette pushed against the wall with her arm twisted behind her back.

"It's a rare power and it's not common knowledge."

By now, they had garnered the attention of the other patrons in the bar. And the big, burly bartender who was approaching Ronan with fury in his fists.

"What is going on here?"

"Where's your security man?" Ronan asked.

The bartender shook his head, then ran over toward the entranceway. He stopped midstride. "He's down."

The woman attacked Ronan again. This time he grabbed her wrists and, binding her arms together, subdued her. "I think they are both very drunk," he said to the bartender.

"Should I call the police?" he asked Ronan.

"Actually, if you have a small locked room, we could just toss them in there until they sober up."

By the way the bartender frowned, Ronan guessed he didn't much like the idea.

"Where's Sallos?" Ivy asked, still trying to keep the brunette pressed against the wall.

Ronan looked around in a panic. "I don't know. I don't see him."

"I'm right here, Ivy, my dear."

Both Ronan and Ivy swung around. Sallos stood grinning by the picturesque floor-to-ceiling windows. He had another patron, a young woman, in his clutches. His hand was around her slender throat and she was dangling above the floor, her feet kicking from the lack of oxygen.

The other patrons moved away from him, eyes widened, hands to mouths, shocked by what they were witnessing. The bartender went to move toward Sallos.

Ronan grabbed his arm. "Don't. He'll kill her."

The bartender stopped, but Ronan could see that it was difficult for him not to try and help. Ronan commended him for that, but his help would surely only kill the woman and most likely him, as well.

Keeping the brunette's arm twisted behind her back, Ivy pulled her over to Ronan. "Here. Take her."

Ronan tried to grab the squirming woman but she managed to get out of Ivy's grasp. She flew at Ivy again, but this time Ivy's patience was gone. She reared back and punched the brunette square in the jaw. It sent the woman to the floor, unconscious.

She then pushed the woman he had under wraps backwards and knocked her in the chin. She went down like a sack of potatoes, too. Problem solved.

"Nice," Ronan said but he suspected Ivy wasn't listening. Her attention was all on Sallos.

She took a few steps toward him. "Let these people go and we'll have a nice long talk."

The demon chuckled. "Oh, is that the part when you kill me?"

"I won't kill you," she mumbled under her breath.

One of Sallos's eyebrows quirked up. "I'm sorry? I don't think I heard you right."

Ronan stepped in beside Ivy. A united front. He hoped it was enough to best this demon. He wasn't so sure, though. Sallos was notorious for his viciousness and manipulations.

"You heard plenty."

"Hmm." Sallos tapped his lips with his finger. "I see a bargain in the near future."

"Whatever," she grunted. "Just let everyone go."

Ronan leaned into her ear. "Are you sure about this? He's a sneaky bastard."

She shook her head. "No, but it's all I got right now."

"If I let everyone go free, Ivy Strom, will you refrain from killing me?"

Ronan could practically hear her teeth grinding. She sighed, and then said, "Yes."

"How about you, Mr. Ames? Care to bargain again?"

Ivy glanced at Ronan, a question on her lips. He shook his head. "You only get one bargain, Sallos. That's the rules."

"Rules, shmules." He smirked. "So be it." Sallos released his hold on the young woman. She dropped to the floor. She didn't look that good. Ronan could see the shallow rise and fall of her chest, but he wasn't sure if that was enough to keep her alive.

He looked over his shoulder to the bartender. "You can help her now. Get her out with the rest of these people."

The bartender nodded, then rushed to the young woman on the floor. He picked her up in his arms and hurried back to the elevators. "Come on! Everyone out!"

That started a stampede for the exits. It wouldn't be long before more security showed up, as well as cops. After a loud, bustling five minutes, Ronan, Ivy and Sallos were alone in The View Lounge. They had to work quickly now.

The demon sat down in the one of the vacant orange chairs and crossed his legs, as if having a casual visit with friends. "So, what shall we talk about?"

Chapter 10

Ivy wanted nothing more than to breach the distance between her and the demon and fry his ass back to hell. But she had made a bargain that she wouldn't kill him. She'd think of a way to get out of it later. In the meantime, there was nothing in there about not hurting him an awful lot.

Sallos gestured to the other two vacant chairs. "Sit. We can talk all night if you'd like."

Ivy moved toward the empty seats but she didn't sit. Ronan moved with her.

Sallos narrowed his eyes at Ronan. "It's been a while, Ronan. You look good."

"How do you know each other?" Ivy asked, curious and suspicious.

"Oh, we go way back, don't we, boy? In fact, I was there at his birth, so to speak."

Ronan stiffened, his hands clenched. "I'll kill you, Sallos. Your bargain isn't with me."

"No one's killing anyone until I get some answers," she said, glaring at Ronan. But she could see the anger and the pain on his face. An urge to console him swept over her, but she tamped it down. At least until their business here was concluded. Obviously, there was a long, painful story there, and surprisingly, she wanted to know it.

Sallos waved his hand. "Ask."

"Where is my brother, Quinn Strom?"

"Ah." He smiled. "There it is. The driving force behind everything you do. The prodigal brother. The chosen one. The great, mighty Quinn Strom."

"Where is he?"

"Why do you want to know? Why do you want to find him?"

"Because he's my brother."

"Yes, but if you find him, wouldn't that mean the reign of Ivy Strom, feared demon hunter, would be over?" He ran a finger over his mouth as if in contemplation. "You'd be number two, once again."

"I don't care." But deep down inside, Ivy did care just a little. She liked being the toughest, most feared hunter around. Quinn had been that guy before he disappeared. And Ivy had sort of inherited the title because of her last name.

She'd earned it, she reminded herself. Over the past three years she'd earned every drop of blood to be called the best. She might have learned her skills from Quinn and her father, but she'd honed them, expanded on them and even perfected them in Quinn's absence.

"Now, I know why Ronan wants to find Quinn Strom, but you, Ivy, my dear, are a different matter altogether."

Ivy glanced at Ronan. "What's he talking about?"

"Nothing. He's trying to manipulate you. He's messing with you."

Sallos waggled his finger. "Now, now, Ronan, don't be lying to the girl. I can tell how much you really like her. Lying is not a good way to start a relationship."

Silver blade in hand, Ronan rushed the demon. He was aiming for Sallos's throat, but the demon was faster and he tossed Ronan across the room like a feather-filled pillow.

Ronan landed on top of the bar, glasses and bottles breaking under and over him until he was lying still in a pool of shattered glass.

"Idiot," Sallos growled. "I'll always be faster than you. You'd think you'd know that by now."

Brushing at the glass, Ronan sat up. "And you should realize by now that I'm smarter."

Sallos went to laugh but then looked down at himself. A devil's trap was stuck to his chest and there was nothing he could do about it. He couldn't tear it off or even touch it, for that matter. He was now bound to the spot and had to, by creed, answer Ivy's questions truthfully.

She grinned. "Looks like you're screwed, Sallos."

The demon glared at Ronan as he stumbled his way back to Ivy's side. There were little cuts on his face and hands. But nothing too serious that would keep him out of action. She imagined it would take a lot to put Ronan down.

"Anything to keep your secrets, hey, boy?"

"Enough of your double-talk, demon," Ivy spit out, "I want to know where my brother is."

Standing, Sallos turned his angry red glare onto her. She could see the fires of hell in the round orbs. He wasn't even bothering to hide his true nature any longer.

"Know that he wasn't taken. He chose to disappear. He chose to leave you, Ivy. He chose to abandon his baby sister for his own design."

She didn't want his words to matter to her, but they needled her regardless. She'd always wondered how he left, and why. Her biggest question, her deepest hurt, was how he could've chosen to leave her completely alone to battle the monsters on her own.

"I don't care. I just want to know where he is. I command you to tell me."

The demon's face began to twist and grimace. "He doesn't want you to find him. Can't you understand that? He doesn't want to see you."

"Tell me!" she yelled.

She knew he was fighting the compulsion. Most demons couldn't fight it. But Sallos was more powerful than that. He was, or had been, a great duke in hell. He commanded legions of demons. So she should've known he would fight it to the end.

And that was when she realized what he intended to do.

She was moving forward even as Sallos turned and ran into the glass window. The force of his motion shattered the glass in front of him and in seconds he was falling to his death.

Ivy jumped across the room, her hand reaching for him. Her fingertips brushed the cotton of his shirt, but when she landed on her stomach, her hand was empty. She'd missed him by a measurement she couldn't even fathom. She'd failed.

But the momentum of her jump had her sliding towards the gaping hole in the thick glass window.

Flailing her arms to stop her fall, she could feel the glass cutting into her skin. Her head was over the edge, and she thought she was going to go over. But she stopped falling.

She looked behind her and saw Ronan with a firm grip on her legs. He had her. By the look in his eyes, he wasn't letting her go for anything. She thanked the Lord for that or she would've been Ivy cream pie on the sidewalk.

He pulled her back a little and she was able to release her grip on the edges of the window. Her hands were bleeding, as were her forearms, but she was alive.

She flipped over onto her back and stared up at Ronan. Tears pricked her eyes, not because she'd almost died, but because she had lost her last chance to find her brother. She'd waited three years for this one, and it had jumped out the window.

Without words, Ronan reached down and helped her to her feet. He nestled her into the crook of his arm. Sirens could be heard from down below on the street. The cops would be here any moment.

"We need to go," Ronan murmured to her as he led her out of the lounge and to the stairwell.

She let him lead her through the hotel. She felt numb, and for the first time in her life, lost. What was she going to do now?

Chapter 11

After he got Ivy out of the lounge and into the stairwell, she perked up and did what needed to be done. Ronan knew she was operating on autopilot but maybe that's what she needed to do to function and survive.

The cops had been swarming up the elevators and stairs when Ronan and Ivy popped out on the twentieth floor and picked up their bags, which had been cleverly hidden near the exit. They cleaned up a bit in a public washroom and wrapped coats over their ruined clothes before heading down in the elevator to the lobby. Still masquerading as the happily married rich couple, they swept through the lobby and out of the hotel without anyone calling foul.

They made it to the truck, parked several blocks away. Ronan took the keys from Ivy, put her in the cab and drove out of the downtown area. She needed a safe place to let go and to finally gather her shit together. So he opted for his place.

It was small, quiet, unassuming and so tucked out of the way that no one would ever even consider that he would live there. Plus it was heavily warded. Nothing could get in. He had some tricks that even Ivy didn't know. Things he'd learned from demons themselves about the art of being invisible.

"Where are we going?" she asked after they were out of the downtown area.

"My place."

"What if it's compromised?"

"It won't be. I fly under the radar. There isn't a target on my back like there is with you. Every demon within a hundred miles of San Francisco is out for your blood. The Stroms have been killing demons for a long time."

She didn't say anything after that, just looked out the side window watching the world zoom by, contemplating her own personal demons, he suspected.

Another ten minutes passed, and she spoke

again, still without looking at him. "What did Sallos mean, he was there at your birth?"

"Ten years ago, I was coming out of a bar, drunk and stupid, thinking I was tough shit, and I was jumped by two men in the alley. Except they weren't men."

She turned and looked at him.

"That was the night I was turned into what I am now. Sallos was there with the other demon. Sallos held me down as the other nearly ripped my throat out." He pulled down the collar of his shirt to show her the six-inch scar that started in the middle of his neck and arced to the left over his thorax. "Instead of killing me, the other demon thought it would be fun to feed me his blood. I was helpless to stop it. It tore open its wrist and held it to my mouth. I tried to spit it out but Sallos made me swallow."

She studied him for a moment. "I'm sorry. I wasn't aware of how it worked. I didn't know that's what happened to you to become a cambion."

He rubbed his face. His skin was clammy from talking about it. "Yeah, you can be born one or made one. Either way you have demon blood racing through your body. Demon blood that won't ever go away."

She stared at him for another few minutes and then turned back to the window. He thought he saw her shiver once, but it could've been from the cool night air circulating through the cab.

After another thirty minutes in the truck, Ronan pulled to the curb and parked. Ivy opened the door and slid out. He came around, grabbed their bags from the bed and led her to his four-story apartment complex.

Without speaking, they climbed the three flights of stairs to the third floor, then walked down the dimly lit corridor. Ronan unlocked his door, threw it open and gestured for her to enter.

His apartment was small and cramped, but it was home. At least it had been for the past year. He tended to move around a lot, as did most people who worked in the dark shadows of life. He wasn't a hunter by trade. He had other qualities that suited him for other lines of work.

Ronan set their bags down near the worn but comfy sofa that dominated the living room. "Sit anywhere. I'll get us some food. There's a great Thai place on the corner."

"I need to shower and change."

He nodded. "You should probably let me look at those cuts on your hands and arms, too."

She shrugged but didn't say anything. He gestured to the short hall off the main room. "It's the first door on your left. There are clean towels under the sink."

She grabbed her bag and walked, head down, to the bathroom.

He was worried about her. The Ivy Strom he'd come to know in such a short period of time wouldn't let anything crush her. She fought back on every front. On fronts she didn't even need to battle. But this woman in his apartment was two steps away from being broken.

Although she was a means to an end for him, he couldn't help the protective feelings surging through him. He wanted to go to her and soothe her, console her. Tell her that everything was going to be okay and that they'd find her brother. That it wasn't how Sallos had described it. That Quinn hadn't abandoned her to her fate.

But he knew on some level that Sallos was truthful. He had to be while compelled by the devil's trap. But he also knew that demons had had millenniums of practice in manipulation. There was the truth and then there was the way a demon spun it.

Ronan went into the little kitchenette, opened one cupboard, took out a bottle of scotch and poured two short glasses. He downed one, then refilled the glass. Picking up the other, he walked the short corridor to the closed bathroom door.

He splayed his hand across the wood and leaned against it. He wished he could sense Ivy's mood.

Would she welcome a shoulder to lean on? Or would she hate him for it? He supposed she wasn't all that fond of him anyway, so it wasn't as if he'd lose much if he pressed the issue.

Taking a deep breath, he turned the knob on the door and went in.

Ivy was in the shower. The spray from the showerhead pounded down on her. She hadn't bothered to pull the flimsy curtain around her and he watched as water rivulets sluiced over her flawless pale flesh. The steam from the hot water floated around her body, giving the illusion that she was hovering on a cloud.

She turned her head under the spray and looked at him. There was no anger, no fury in those eyes. He saw loss and pain and a vulnerability he'd never thought to see in her.

He knew he should've turned and walked out. The right thing to do would be to leave her to her sorrow. But he also knew he wasn't going to.

He handed her the drink. "I thought you might need this."

She took the glass and downed the alcohol in one gulp. She handed him back the glass, which he set on the sink.

He stared at her, feeling like a cad for drinking in his fill of her incredible body, but she made no move to cover herself or to pull the curtain shut.

"Do you want me to leave?" he asked, his voice tight with desire and other emotions he couldn't quite label. Or maybe didn't want to quite yet.

She shook her head, water droplets flying off her skin with the movement.

Ronan stripped off his shirt and tossed it to the floor. He then undid his pants and shucked them off, kicking them aside. He was naked underneath and aroused.

As he stepped into the shower next to her, his body slid up against hers. The muscles in his gut clenched at the slight contact.

Without words, she opened her arms to him and he settled his body against hers. She wrapped her hands behind his neck and found his mouth with fierce urgency. She kissed him hard, with frantic nibbles on his lips, and sucked at his tongue.

He wrapped his arms around her and let her take him the way she wanted, the way she needed. The control was hers. If he couldn't give her a shoulder to cry on, he could give her this.

Breaking from the kiss, Ivy stepped out of the shower, pulling him out with her. She pushed him down onto the closed toilet. Before he could do anything, she was straddling his lap.

"Ivy, we—"

"Don't talk. I don't need any words. I just need this."

Then she was kissing him again, her fingers buried in his hair, pulling on his head as she peppered kisses to his chin and down to his throat.

Wrapping his hands around her firm rear end, he lifted her up a little, then settled her back down onto the hot, hard length of his erection. The second he entered her, he was on fire. He was burning alive from the inside out. And when she started to move on him, at first slow and tortuous then gaining her rhythm and finally breaking into a frantic pace, Ronan thought he'd incinerate to ashes.

Ivy squeezed her eyes shut and grabbed onto his shoulders as she rode him hard. She'd never been so frenzied before when it came to sex. But the second she'd seen him framed in the open bathroom doorway she knew he was exactly what she needed. He was her perfect fix. To take the pain away. To take the thoughts and feelings of loneliness and abandonment from her heart. If only for a moment. It was enough, to trade her pain in for the rushing, surging, fiery passion she was fueling now, even though she knew the furious sizzling sensations wouldn't last.

It was a temporary fix to a long-festering problem.

She dug her fingers in and rode him harder and faster. She opened her eyes and looked down into his face. He met her gaze and it was as fierce and hard as the feelings rippling inside her were. He was a strong man, Ronan. Strong enough for her. At least for now.

Leaning down, she found his mouth and kissed him. His hands streaked up her back and burrowed into her hair. Holding her head, he tilted her slightly and deepened the kiss. His tongue clashed against hers, no longer teasing. He nipped at her lips then moved down to her chin, to trail his tongue up and down her throat. He suckled on her skin, coaxing moans from her lips.

Quivers erupted in her thighs as she slammed down on him. The muscles in her belly tightened and she knew she was so close to coming. Wrapping her arms around his head, she pressed him to her breasts while pumping him fast and hard, almost remorseless in her movements. She was after only one thing. Release.

Release from her thoughts, release from her anger and pain.

She needed that freedom from her mind to stay sane.

Ivy slammed down on him once, twice, three more times until the orgasm exploded inside her. She cried out and dug her fingers into his scalp.

She could feel his hands on her hips, clutching her tight. So tight it almost hurt. But she took that pain and twirled it around into pleasure. She floated on it, as it spun her around and around. Her head was dizzy, and her heart thumped so hard she could barely breathe.

She tried to pull up away from him, but Ronan yanked her down and held her still, anchored to him as he followed her down into the sizzling-hot center of the storm.

Chapter 12

Ronan blinked into the morning light casting from his bedroom window. He sat up in bed and slowly swung his legs over the side. He glanced over his shoulder at Ivy's sleeping form to make sure he hadn't woken her. Her eyes were still closed, her hands tucked up under her chin. He watched her chest. Her breathing was slow and steady. Relief flooded him that she still slept.

After their sex bout in the bathroom, Ronan had picked her up and brought her into the bedroom. He'd laid her down, snuggled in behind her, pulled the covers over them and held her tight until she fell asleep. They hadn't spoken a word to each other. He supposed they hadn't needed to. What was there to say?

The sex had been therapeutic for them both. It had provided an avenue for Ivy to escape and a way for Ronan to offer her sympathy. He still felt like a heel for taking advantage of her anguish, but it couldn't be helped. There had been no way in hell he could've walked away from her.

It might not have been the smartest thing for either of them to do, considering their circumstances and positions, but sometimes what's smart and what's needed are two entirely different things.

He reached for a pair of sweatpants and pulled them on. Once dressed, he left the bedroom, quietly shut the door behind him and padded into the living room. His stomach rumbled. He was starving. He hadn't gotten around to ordering any food last night.

He went to the refrigerator and opened it. Inside it was nearly empty. He managed to find an apple, a chunk of cheese and a can of soda. He cut the apple, leaving half for Ivy, and then wolfed it down with half the cheese block and a few healthy sips of soda.

Chewing, he sank onto the sofa and thought about what a mess he was in and how the hell he could get out of it. He suspected when Ivy found out the true nature of his mission, she wouldn't be forgiving.

He had to tell her, 'fess up before she found out on her own. When he'd agreed to his mission, he hadn't foreseen developing feelings for the ice-queen hunter. But he had. In spades.

So he'd finish his apple, then go in and wake her up to tell her the real reason he'd shown up in the back alley of that club to accidentally bump into one of the most infamous demon hunters around.

But he didn't get a chance before there was a knock on his front door.

He usually didn't get visitors. He didn't know his neighbors and he didn't have any friends—at least none who would make social visits.

Cautiously, he made his way to the door. He peered through the peephole. The hallway beyond his door was empty. That didn't necessarily mean anything.

Another knock came, harder this time. Louder.

Ronan glanced over his shoulder to his closed bedroom door, hoping the noise hadn't woken Ivy.

"Open up, Ronan, or I'll break it down," came a snooty cultured voice. A voice he unfortunately knew all too well.

Sighing heavily, he unhooked the chain, threw the bolt and pulled open the door.

Reginald Watson, one of the most powerful sorcerers in San Francisco, waltzed into his apartment, his gaze darting all around, his nose in the air.

"What do you want?" Ronan asked.

"To make sure you're still doing your job."

"You could've used the phone, Reggie."

The sorcerer winced at Ronan's shortened use of his name. He sniffed. "I have been. You've been ignoring my calls."

"I know my job. You don't need to be looking over my shoulder. That wasn't part of our deal."

"What is part of your deal?"

Ronan cursed under his breath, then swung around to see Ivy leaning on the wall in the corridor. She had on one of his T-shirts; the hem skimmed her midthigh.

Reginald looked at Ronan and grinned. It was a smile that said, "You've been caught."

"When I told you to hook up with Ivy Strom, I didn't realize you had this in mind."

Ronan turned and launched at Reginald, but the sorcerer had anticipated the attack. He threw up a protective shield in front of him with his magic. Ronan bounced off the hard purple defense shield like a rubber ball against cement.

"Don't get all bent out of shape, Ronan. You wouldn't want me to change our arrangement, would you? Out of a case of bad judgment on your part."

Ivy strode into the room, her hands balled into fists as her side. "Someone better tell me what the fuck is going on before I lose it."

Ronan picked himself off the floor and slumped onto the sofa. He ran a shaky hand through his hair, and then looked at her. "The Crimson Hall Cabal is paying me to help you find your brother."

"Why? What do they want him for?"

Reginald cleared his throat, as if he was auditioning for a play and not destroying Ronan's morning. "Quinn is in possession of something very important. An item the cabal desires."

"What?"

"A key."

Ivy glared at the sorcerer. "Look, dickwad, I don't know who you are and I really don't care, but quit jerking me around and tell me the whole deal."

Ronan tracked her gaze and he could see the fury and the pain there. He couldn't save her from it. "The key opens a chest that supposedly contains the grimoire from which King Solomon conjured his seventy-two demons to do his bidding."

She cocked one eyebrow. "You're serious?"

"Yes, unfortunately."

"And you're getting paid to do this? How much are they paying you to screw me?"

He dropped his gaze and looked at the floor. "Enough." He didn't want to tell her what he was really doing it for. Let her think the worst of him. It would be easier that way.

"Oh, don't be so hard on him, my dear. He's just doing what he's always done. Survive. It's really what we all are doing, don't you think?"

She glared at Reginald. Ronan could see something glinting from her cupped hand. He was up off the sofa and grabbing her arm before she could cross the room and bury the hidden blade into the sorcerer's chest.

She tried to struggle out of his hold, but he used his demon strength to keep her still. "Don't be foolish. Killing him would only bring the cabal down on your head."

"I wasn't going to kill him. Just hurt him a little."

Reginald chuckled. "I can see why you're smitten, Ronan. She's charming." The sorcerer made his way back to the door. "Well, I should be off. Thanks for the visit, Ronan. It's a pleasure, as always." He opened the door, and stepped out, then paused. "Oh, and please start answering your phone. I really don't want to come back here." He slammed the door shut.

When he was gone, Ronan let Ivy go. She moved away from him, but didn't make any move to disarm herself. He imagined that she thought of sliding that knife into him.

"I'm sorry you had to find out like this," he said.

"Were you planning on telling me you're using me to get to my brother and steal this key from him?"

He looked at her for a long moment, cautious with his next words. "Not at first."

She turned on her heel and headed back to the bedroom, most likely with the intention of getting dressed and getting the hell out of his apartment. He couldn't let her go, and not just because he needed to find Quinn.

Ronan chased after her. "But I was planning to before Reggie showed up. Things have changed between us, and I wanted to be truthful. Before you were just a job, but now…"

She swung around and poked him in the chest with the hilt of her blade. "Now, what? Now, we're in love?" The sarcasm dripped from her voice like venom from a snake's fang. "We had sex, Ronan. That's it. Mindless, thoughtless sex. I had an itch and you scratched it." She lowered the knife. "So thanks for that."

He never thought another human being could hurt him again. But he was wrong. Ivy's words sliced him to the bone.

Nodding, he took a step back from her. "Right. Great. You're welcome. So shall we continue this arrangement, or do you want to bail?"

Her eyes widened. He suspected she thought he would say something different, respond to her icy demeanor with maybe pleas for forgiveness, but that's not how he played. He didn't supplicate anyone.

"I'm not bailing."

"Fine. Then we'll reconvene in the living room once you get dressed and get your moods under control. Then we'll work on finding your brother." With that, he turned and walked out of the bedroom, leaving her gaping at him like a fish.

Appalled, Ivy watched him leave the room. She itched to chase after him and tell him what he could do with that last statement. But she knew if she did she might do something she would regret later. She was feeling sore and hurtful and she wanted to lash out at Ronan.

He'd hurt her in more ways than one. In ways she didn't even realize she could feel pain. Quinn had been right. She couldn't trust any other man in her life. She was way better off alone.

The sex had been cathartic for her, though. She'd needed to feel something other than the confusion and hurt that pounded in her head and heart. She took Ronan's presence in the bathroom as an offering to help her ease her pain. Instinctively he had known she wouldn't have accepted kind words and a gentle hug. She needed physical contact with someone. She'd wanted it from Ronan.

She couldn't deny it had been fierce and passionate and explosive. Even now she could feel his flesh in her hands and between her thighs. Her gut clenched at the thought of having sex with him again. It had been a long time since she'd been with a man. And even longer since she'd had any romantic feelings for one.

She was the love-'em-and-leave-'em type. She didn't have room in her life for anyone. She couldn't worry about someone else's welfare. She had to look after herself, physically, mentally and spiritually. She needed to be fully intact to do the job she did. Having feelings for someone just opened up those avenues. Avenues where pain could sneak through and attack. She had enough creatures attacking her on a daily basis; she didn't need her own thoughts and feelings doing the same.

She grabbed her bag, zipped it open and took out a pair of jeans and a long-sleeved T-shirt. As she dressed, she thought about how angry she was at Ronan for lying to her, for keeping his true motives a secret. But truth be told, it really didn't change anything. Not in the big picture. He wanted to help her find Quinn. That hadn't changed. He had resources she didn't have access to. That hadn't changed. So what was the real issue here?

And why did it still sting right in the middle of her chest?

She finished dressing, determined not to show any more emotion. Her dad had been the one to drill it into her head about the weakness of showing emotions. They slowed a person down. Sometimes even stopping them from doing what needed to be done.

She wouldn't let that happen. Her goal was to find Quinn, and nothing from this moment forward was going to stop her from doing that. No matter what came her way, she would keep her resolve and do what was required. Even if that meant leaving Ronan behind.

Chapter 13

The tempting smells of hot food drifted to Ivy's nose as she made her way out of the bedroom and back to the living room. Ronan was already seated, eating something that smelled delicious out of a white cardboard box.

He gestured toward the rest of the smorgasbord spread out on the table. "It's from this Thai restaurant down the block. Eat it. It's good."

She was hungry enough that she didn't see the point of arguing. She grabbed a box, some chopsticks, secured a comfy spot on the floor and dug in.

They ate in silence and she didn't look at Ronan until she was done her food. She tossed the empty box onto the table, then pinned him with her gaze. He glanced up at her from shoveling noodles into his mouth.

"I want to know more about this key."

He nodded and wiped his mouth with the back of his hand. "I've set up an appointment with a contact of mine. She's a demonologist and knows everything there is to know about King Solomon and his grimoire."

"When?"

"In an hour."

She stood and started back toward the bedroom. "It'll give me time to sharpen my knives."

"Ivy…"

She stopped but didn't turn around to face him. "We don't need to talk about it. It doesn't matter."

"For what it's worth, I'm sorry I lied to you. And I'm sorry if I hurt you."

"You didn't." Then she kept going into the bedroom, shutting the door firmly behind her. She leaned against the wood and fought back the hot prickles at the corners of her eyes. She wouldn't let the tears fall. And she'd be damned if she ever let Ronan see her cry, especially because of him.

She balled her hands tightly, digging her nails into her palms, and took in a few deep breaths. She would put on her mask and show him it didn't matter, that he didn't matter. It would be one of the hardest things she'd ever done, but she'd do it, just as she always had.

Forty-five minutes later, they were back in the truck, racing down the highway toward San Francisco State University. Ronan's contact was a woman named Quianna Lang who was a professor in the humanities department. Supposedly, she was a guru on all world religions, with a slant toward demonology.

They parked in visitor parking and crossed the campus to the gray humanities building. They went in and up to the fourth floor to Quianna's office. Ronan knocked on the closed door.

"Come in," a youngish female voice sounded from within.

Ronan opened the door and he and Ivy stepped into the cramped office. The woman behind the desk stood and came around to them. She was a petite woman, with a warm smile but cold, hard eyes. Ivy wondered what she'd seen in her life to give her that fierce gaze.

"Ronan." She embraced him with a familiarity that almost grated on Ivy's spine. She shook off the feeling and met the woman head-on.

"This is Ivy Strom," Ronan said. "Ivy, this is Quianna Lang."

The little woman held out her hand to Ivy. She shook it and Ivy noticed Quianna had a firm, solid grip even with her dainty-looking hand. "It's a pleasure, of course, to meet you, Ivy. I've heard a lot about you and your family."

Ivy just nodded, unsure how she felt about the woman. She gave Ivy an unsettling feeling. Like she'd just walked through a cold spot or someone's restless spirit.

"I met your father once."

"Really?" Ivy cocked one eyebrow.

"Yes." Quianna sat on the edge of her desk, and then turned to regard Ronan. "So why the meeting?"

"We need to know all you know about Solomon's grimoire and the key to the chest that supposedly holds it."

Quianna's face paled. "Are you serious?"

Ronan nodded. "Supposedly Quinn Strom has the key."

"And?" She looked from Ronan to Ivy and back to Ronan.

"And the Crimson Hall Cabal have hired this one—" she gestured to Ronan "—to find it and bring it to them," Ivy added, loving that the little demonologist just fixed Ronan with a lethal stare worthy of any deadly hunter. She was impressed.

"You dumb ass." Quianna slid off the desk and went toe-to-toe with him, although she was a good seven inches shorter. "You can't give them the key.

If they find the chest and open it, you can't even imagine the power that will be unleashed."

"Don't you think you're being a bit overdramatic?" he asked.

Quianna swatted Ronan on the side of the head. "Don't you think you're the dumbest man on earth?"

Ivy broke out into laughter. To see the little spitfire cuff a big man like Ronan had tickled her silly. Because the look on his face, one of astonishment, was priceless to see.

Quianna turned to Ivy. "You seem like an intelligent woman. Can't you talk some sense into him?"

Ivy put up her hand in defense. "I don't own him. He's his own person. I just want to find my brother. I don't really give a shit about the rest of it."

"Well, you should." She sat back on the edge of her desk. "Did you ever stop to think why your brother disappeared? Maybe it was to hide the key. To keep it from evil hands, like the Crimson Hall Cabal."

"Do you know where he went?" Ivy stepped toward her, suddenly frantic to know something, anything. Any tiny straw would do to grasp.

Quianna shook her head. "I don't. And even if I did, I don't think I'd tell either of you."

Ronan sighed. "Qui, just tell us about the key. Let us deal with the morality of finding it."

She looked at him, then at Ivy and shook her head. "I don't think either one of you would know morality even if it hit you in the face."

Ivy had to admit she was probably right, but she certainly didn't like to hear it so simply stated. As if it was obvious just by looking at her. "Look, lady, you don't know me, so keep your opinions about my character to yourself."

Quianna frowned, then shrugged. "Fair enough." She slid off the desk again and went around to slump into her high-backed leather chair. She spun it around to her bookcase, pulled out a huge black-encased tome and slammed it down on her desk. She flipped through the pages. Then, settling on one, she turned the book around and slid it toward them. "This is what the key looks like."

Ivy and Ronan gazed down at the open book. On the left page was a pencil drawing of an elaborately decorated key, not unlike something from the past. A skeleton key. On the opposite page was a drawing of a plain wooden chest.

Quianna tapped the paper. "This chest supposedly holds the grimoire that King Solomon used to conjure his demons."

"Where's the chest?" Ronan asked.

"Nobody knows."

"So essentially the key is useless unless you know where the chest is," Ivy stated.

Quianna met her gaze, and there was something inside her cold gray eyes that sent a shiver down Ivy's back. "Theoretically, yes."

"Thanks for the info, Qui." Ronan looked at Ivy. "Let's go."

Ivy nodded and followed Ronan to the door. Before they crossed the threshold, Quianna gave them a warning. "You don't know what you are messing with, Ronan. You think you know what real evil looks like? You have no clue. Those who open the grimoire will be cursed for life."

Both Ivy and Ronan looked over their shoulders at the professor. She'd risen from her chair and was staring after them with a look of determination on her thin pale face.

"Give the key to the cabal and you risk your immortal soul."

"Too late," Ronan said. "I lost it the night I was turned into a demon." He swung back around and left the office.

Ivy watched him go, not fully realizing until this very moment how damaged he was from being turned into a cambion. She knew he struggled with it, but had no clue how much he loathed his very existence.

And now she understood his motives for wanting to find her brother. He was going to trade the key for something that would turn him back into a full-blooded human. She didn't blame him for it. She'd likely do the exact same thing.

"He's going to need your help, Ivy," Quianna murmured. "At the end."

"What? Have you seen the future?"

"Yes, actually, I have."

Ivy frowned. "I've never met anyone with that ability before."

"Yeah, well, now you have." Quianna sat back in her chair and cocked one eyebrow at her. "Believe me, if I could turn it off, I would. The future isn't looking too good. I can't tell you more than that."

Unnerved, Ivy nodded to Quianna, then walked out of the office to follow a man she was just beginning to understand but couldn't be more confused about.

Chapter 14

They didn't talk as they made their way back to the truck. Ivy claimed the driver's seat, and as they pulled out of the parking lot she glanced at Ronan. "Your friend is a bit intense."

He nodded. "Yeah, but she knows a lot."

"She may have a lot of information, but she doesn't know everything."

Ronan turned and looked at Ivy. She gave him a half smile. And right there he knew she'd accepted his apology and that they were back to being on an even keel.

He returned her smile, then looked out the side window. Quianna had been right about him, though. His morality would be in question if he gave the key to the cabal. He had heard rumors about the grimoire but never thought it was real. Just an old myth to scare people. And he admitted it worked. The thought of that book being in the hands of immoral beings like Reginald Watson frightened him to the core. But it wasn't the book he was supposed to deliver, it was only the key. A key that was useless without something to unlock.

This was his one and only chance to be normal again. The cabal had a cure to his cambionism, a cure for the blood poisoning him every second of every day. Exchange the key for a cure. He'd do anything for that opportunity. He'd do anything to be human again, including stealing the key from Quinn Strom. They just had to find him first.

As Ivy pulled out onto the major highway that would lead them back toward his place, her cell phone jingled from her jacket pocket. She retrieved it and flipped it open. "Yeah?" While she listened, she nodded, then glanced at Ronan. It must've been the call they were waiting for.

"Okay, see you in a few." She flipped the phone closed and slid it back into her pocket. "That was Jake. He has a lead. We're going to meet him down in the Castro."

"The Castro?"

She shrugged. "I don't know. Didn't ask. Don't care."

Ivy parked the truck on Market Street and they got out and walked up to Castro Street and to the historic Castro Theatre. Ronan normally didn't visit the area, famed for its diverse gay community, but he had been to the theatre once before when they were playing the director's cut of *Blade Runner,* one of his favorite movies.

He loved the look of the theatre—old-school movie going with elegance and extravagance. The chandelier in the main movie hall made him think of the nostalgic era of Hollywood when movie stars were untouchable, classy and cool. Not like today, he thought.

Ivy bought two tickets to the show at the round ticket booth out front and they went in. She nodded toward the left staircase. "He said he'd meet us on the balcony."

As they ascended the stairs, Ronan said, "Seems like a strange place for a meeting."

"It's dark, it's private and no one would ever think to look for us here. So I think it's damn near perfect."

He chuckled at that. She was right.

The balcony was empty save for one person near the overhang. As they approached, Ronan could see that Jake was a pretty big dude—bulging muscles under a tight black T-shirt and denim jeans. He looked like an army commando; he even had the buzz cut to go with it.

He lifted a hand to Ivy as they neared, then his face changed and he was rushing up the aisle with a knife in his hand, right toward Ronan.

Ivy must've noticed it the same time Ronan did, because she was jumping in front of Jake, her hands on his chest. "Wait. Stop."

He pushed past her and reached for Ronan. But Ronan was faster and he jumped clear over two rows of seats and away from the bruiser.

"He's a demon, Ivy."

Ivy smacked him in the chest with the palm of her hand. "He's not full-blooded. He's a cambion. And he's with me."

Jake lowered his knife, but didn't sheath it. "Never knew you to be soft toward the hellspawn."

Ronan's hands fisted. He had a violent urge to pummel the guy into the ground. Jake reminded Ronan of all the hunters he'd dealt with over the years. Arrogant and ignorant.

At first he'd thought of Ivy that way. But as he'd gotten to know her a little, he realized she was far more intelligent and multifaceted than anyone he'd met before.

"He's not hellspawn. I suggest you keep your opinions of things you know nothing of to yourself in the future." She poked him in the chest. "I like you, Jake, but not that much."

Jake looked at Ronan one last time, then sheathed his blade back under his shirt. "It's your rep on the line. Not mine." He returned to his perch at the edge of the balcony overhang.

She followed him there as Ronan came around the rows of seats to set up a position along the railing, close enough that he could hear what was going on but not where Jake could take a cheap shot at him.

"So what do you have?" Ivy asked.

Jake handed her a folded piece of white paper. "My sources tell me that your brother was seen at this address."

She took it and opened it up. "Where is this?"

"Washington."

"Are you sure this is legit?"

He nodded. "Yeah. I'm sure."

"How long ago was he seen?"

"About two weeks."

"So he could've moved on."

Jake shrugged. "Sure. You know Quinn. He doesn't stay in one place for long."

Ivy pocketed the note. "Thanks, Jake. I appreciate it." She held out her hand to him.

He shook it, then glanced in Ronan's direction. "Are you sure about him?"

Ivy met Ronan's gaze. He could feel her probing stare even in the dark. Her eyes were that piercing. Finally, she nodded. "Yeah, I'm sure."

"Okay. I'll keep your liaison to myself."

She snorted. "I don't give a shit if you tell everyone. I know what I know, and that's all that matters to me." With that she headed back down the aisle. Ronan fell into step beside her.

They didn't talk until they were back outside and headed toward the truck.

"Do you trust the lead?" he asked.

"Going to have to. Jake's usually a stand-up guy, plus it's the only thing we got to go on."

"So, to Washington, hey?"

She shrugged. "Looks like it. We'll go back to your place, pack our gear and head out. If we drive all day and night, we could make it there by tomorrow night."

He nodded. "Okay." He paused with his hand on the handle of the passenger door. "Are you sure you still want to find your brother with me? I could end up causing a ton of problems."

She looked at him for a long moment, then shrugged. "You already have. Besides, you're not bad company. You at least know how to fight. So that's something." She opened her door and got in, but not before he caught the slight twitch of her lips.

Chapter 15

The sun was low in the sky as Ivy took the ramp from the I-80 E onto the I-5 N. They were almost four hours out of San Francisco and heading into Oregon. The trip so far had been quiet. Neither of them had really spoken much. Although deep down, Ivy had a ton to say. She just didn't know what words to put together.

Something had definitely changed between them. Twice. And she wasn't sure how she felt about any of it.

Best to keep her true thoughts to herself. Once they found Quinn, Ronan would get what he wanted and disappear. She had no doubt about that. Besides, it was best for everyone if he did.

It wasn't as if they were going to become friends, or partners, or...

Best to let it go. Best to let him go.

Seeing Jake's reaction to Ronan's presence made it clear to Ivy that her and Ronan's liaison would not go unnoticed. And that the hunting community might not be so accepting of it. A community that she'd been part of since she took her first steps and spoke her first word.

Which just happened to be demon.

Mind made up, she drove in silence, every now and then changing the radio station to get something decent to listen to. Thankfully, that was one thing she and Ronan had in common, an eclectic taste in music from Motown to Metallica.

"Do you want me to drive?" Ronan asked. "You can catch some sleep. You look like you're going to hit your forehead on the wheel any second."

"No, I'm not." She yawned. Then rolled her eyes. "Fine." She pulled over onto the shoulder and parked the truck.

There was virtually no traffic on the road. She opened her door and jumped out to come around as Ronan just slid across the seat. Once she was back in, she fastened her seat belt and balled up her black hoodie. She crammed it in against the side window and leaned her head against it. "Wake me in a few hours to switch back."

Ronan put the truck in Drive and pulled back onto the road. Ivy closed her eyes and willed herself to sleep. She was usually pretty good about sleeping in various spots, having been on the road all her life. She could basically put her head down anywhere she felt safe and fall asleep.

And she was just about asleep when Ronan yanked the truck to the shoulder and squealed to a stop.

Her eyes flashed open. "What the hell?"

"Get out of the truck!" he shouted, just as he flung open the driver's door and jumped out.

"What..." Then she saw the look in his eyes and remembered the incident in her garage. Without another word, she threw open her door and jumped out. She grabbed her bag from behind the seat just as Ronan was tossing their gear out from the bed of the truck.

"Take what you can and run!"

He snatched up as much he could. She helped him with the rest and they ran out into an open field. Ivy jammed her foot between two large rocks and took a hard spill to the ground. Ronan stopped and turned, running to her even as she scrambled to her feet. But her left ankle had taken a twist and couldn't support her full weight.

"Go. I'll follow," she grunted as she tried to put

pressure on her foot, wincing as the pain zipped up her leg like electricity.

Ronan dumped his personal bag and picked her up without any effort. He started to run with her in his arms.

"Don't be stupid. You can't—"

But her words were drowned out by the deafening boom of the truck exploding behind them. The force of the blast blew them forward. Ronan lost his footing and they both met the ground hard.

The heat wave blasted over them. Ivy could hear the sizzle of the ends of her hair burning. Before she pushed to her feet, Ronan patted at her head to stop the sizzle from turning into more. Then he was beside her, also getting to his feet, his arm around her, helping her. Once up, they grabbed their bags and continued running from the explosion.

Ivy looked back once over her shoulder. Her truck was completely engulfed in flames. It wasn't the normal orange-and-red fire but had the green tinge of hellfire. Again, someone had tried to kill her and Ronan. And would have succeeded if it hadn't been for Ronan's keen ability to sense it coming mere seconds before it did.

"We need to get out of here before the cops show up." Ronan gestured toward a copse of trees in the distance. "We can make it if we run."

Ivy tested her ankle. It was definitely sprained. Possibly broken after her second spill to the ground. "Maybe if you carried all the gear. I could keep up."

"I could carry you."

She shook her head; sweat from the heat blast and from the pain swimming through her skull flicked off her forehead. "I can do it."

He stared at her for a moment, searching her face, and then nodded. "Okay." He took the bags from her and wrapped the straps around his shoulders so he could carry them on his back. Then he hefted the others over his shoulders and started to run toward the trees.

Ivy followed him. At first, she put her full weight on both feet. Pure agony seared her calves and shins and thighs every time she took a step. It felt like her flesh was on fire underneath her skin. Gritting her teeth and digging her nails into her palms, she put her head down and plowed forward. Sweat dripped from her face and soaked her armpits. The back of her T-shirt was plastered to her skin by the time she was halfway to the trees. She could see that Ronan had already made it.

Determined not to fail, she pressed on, putting one foot in front of the other. But she was putting less pressure on her left foot. She couldn't help it. Her brain was succumbing to the pain she inflicted on it with her foolish running. It was fighting against her.

She could hear the high-pitched whine of sirens in the background. She imagined she would probably be able to see the red-and-blue lights down the highway if she turned and looked over her shoulder. But she continued on. She had to get to the trees before anyone spotted her. It was twilight and she was wearing black, so it would be harder to spot her in the field, but she knew some state troopers had sharp eyes.

Tears streaked her cheeks. She couldn't keep them from rolling from her eyes. The pain was like a part of her now. A constant throb that seemed to ignite every part of her body. To endure much more, she felt like she might puke. She wiped at the sweat trickling into her eyes and kept on moving. She focused on the first tree in the copse. That was all she could see as she limped along the field.

Then she was floating. The pressure on her ankle disappeared, sweet relief spilled over her body and she sighed. Wiping at her eyes, she realized that she wasn't floating but that Ronan had swept her up and was running full speed.

She didn't argue this time. Instead she wrapped her arm around his neck and let him do what needed to be done despite her stubbornness.

Within another minute they were well hidden inside the clump of trees.

He carefully set her down on a sizeable boulder. "Let me look at it."

She shook her head. "Wait until we're somewhere safer."

"Ivy, you can't even walk on it. It needs to be looked at right now or we won't be able to get somewhere safer."

Resigned, she huffed, "Fine."

Ronan knelt down in front of her and unlaced her army boot. She had to grit her teeth as he pulled it off. Once it was gone, more relief set in. But then she looked down. Her white sock was bloodied.

She cursed under her breath.

So did Ronan as he peeled the sock down. He winced when it was almost off. "Your bone is broken."

"Are you sure?"

"Yeah, I'm sure, because a piece of it is sticking out of your skin."

She cursed again, louder this time. She'd known the second she saw the blood on her sock. A person didn't bleed from a simple sprain or break. Only if the skin broke.

"I can fix it, but I need room to work, and you'll need to lie down."

"How can you fix it?"

He rubbed his hands together as if they were cold and he was warming them up. After a second or two, a light blue glow emitted from between his palms. Her eyes widened.

He stopped rubbing and set them to his sides. "More of my awesome demon powers."

She heard the sarcasm in his voice, but if he could heal her with just his hands, she thought his demon powers were, in fact, quite awesome. He'd already used them to save her life, not once but twice. He had no idea how some people would kill to have amazing powers like that. The power to save lives. But she kept those thoughts to herself, knowing he wouldn't appreciate them. He loathed himself too much to see the good inside.

She nodded. "Okay. Where to, then?"

He stood and gestured to the north. "I saw a farmhouse just past these trees. We can try there."

"What if it's occupied?"

"Then you can use that winning personality of yours to charm them into letting us stay the night." He picked up one of the bags. "I can carry you to the bushes along the driveway, check out the situation then come back for the bags."

She wanted to argue, wanted to refuse, but she was realistic enough to admit that she couldn't walk on her ankle at all. She nodded, and he bent down and scooped her up again.

She put her arm around his neck as he walked her out of the trees and over a field to the farm-house in the near distance. From this close prox-imity she could clearly see the dark gray flecks in his stunning eyes. His eyes never failed to make the little hairs on her arms sway to attention. She loved it when he set his gaze on her, studying her. It made her insides pulse pleasantly.

It didn't take him long to reach the row of high bushes that lined the driveway up to the farm-house. He set her down gently, then crouched be-side her to observe the house.

It looked to be over sixty years old, with fading wood along the side, once white, now gray with age. The shingles on the roof were curled and flak-ing as if they'd seen many hailstorms over the vast years. The front had a veranda, and there was an old rocking chair out front. The house was right out of a forgotten era.

"There are no vehicles in the yard." He squinted in the waning light. "No lights on, either."

"There could be a garage around back, and they could be an old couple who went to bed early."

"It's our best bet." He looked around the area. "And frankly our only option right now."

She nodded. She knew he was right.

"Hang tight. I'll get the gear, then I'll give the house a closer look." Then he was off running back to the trees.

Ivy shuffled a little on her behind, trying to get more comfortable. Her ankle felt like it was on fire. She'd had plenty of injuries over the years. A person didn't hunt demons and expect to walk away unscathed. But she'd never broken a bone before. She'd been cut, slashed, stabbed once in the hand, burned, beaten and nearly had her head smashed in by an explosive wrath demon with a hammer. All those things had hurt like hell, but this pain shooting up her leg was something else altogether.

Gritting her teeth, she turned slightly so she could study the farmhouse. It didn't look occupied at the moment, but that didn't mean the owners couldn't return soon. She'd really hate to be caught inside when they did. It wasn't that she was opposed to breaking and entering; heck, she'd committed a long list of unlawful offenses that would likely see her in jail for years. She just didn't want to hurt anyone else if she didn't have to. Civilians always ended up getting in the way, and despite her hard-assed reputation, she didn't like to see innocents suffer needlessly. Contrary to what everyone thought of her, she did possess a heart.

Ronan was back next to her, setting down the gear. He searched her face. "Are you doing okay?"

"I'll live."

"I'll do a recon on the house then come back for you." Then he was gone again.

She watched him as he approached the house. He was fast but cautious, always careful to stay hidden in the darkest shadows. He would've made a good hunter, she thought. He was smart, strong, patient and quick on his feet. And as she was discovering, so much more than that.

It was these other qualities—compassion, protectiveness and the intense way he looked at her—that she noticed about him and it troubled her.

At first, she'd seen nothing but the demon inside Ronan, but now all she could focus on was the man simmering inside. He was a man she knew her dad would've respected, and that was saying something. Her dad hadn't valued many, and he called even fewer friends.

And maybe, just maybe, he might've given his blessing about their...

Relationship?

She shook her head to clear it. She must've been in more pain than she thought if she was labeling her and Ronan's combative yet passionate back-and-forth a relationship.

But if not one, what the hell were they doing?

Chapter 16

After a few minutes, he was back at her side. "Looks clear. Some of the furniture has been covered with sheets. Doesn't look like anyone's been inside for weeks. The grass is overgrown around the deck. It hasn't been mowed in a while."

Ivy nodded. "Let's get inside."

He helped her to her feet, then was about to lift her again when she shook her head. "No, I'll walk."

"Ivy, this is no time for heroics. You're not proving anything to anyone except that you are a stubborn idiot."

"Just grab the gear." She started toward the house, hobbling on her one good ankle.

She didn't want him to carry her. She didn't want to have to rely on him. On her own for years, without someone to lean on, Ivy felt weak and vulnerable in his arms. Two things she hated most.

He didn't argue with her but picked up their bags and followed her down the drive. By the time she got to the front deck, sweat slicked her skin. Her clothes stuck to her back and chest. She grabbed the railing and climbed the stairs, careful not to puke from the pain pulsing through her body.

At the top, Ronan came up next to her and settled by the front door. He leaned down and squeezed the doorknob. There was an audible click and he pushed it open.

Ivy hobbled inside. He followed her in, carrying in their gear. He set it down, then found her a chair and pulled it up so she could sit in the front foyer.

"I'll find a room on the first floor. No sense in climbing those stairs needlessly. Especially if we need to get out fast." He did a quick sweep of the house and came back two minutes later. "There's a den at the back, looks like it has a hide-a-bed."

He helped her to her feet, and then half carried her to the back of the house. He kicked open the door and brought her through. He set her on the edge of the easy chair, then went about tossing cushions off the sofa to pull out the bed inside.

Once the mattress was unfolded, he picked her up and settled her onto it.

His command of her made her feel like a child. She hated that the pain coursing through her made her inept to function on her own.

"Lie down."

"Why?"

"So I can fix your damn leg."

"Why can't you do it while I sit up?"

He fixed her with an intense stare. "Because you need to be absolutely still and it's going to hurt like hell."

"Fine." She plopped onto her back, embarrassed that she'd forgotten why they'd come to the house to begin with. Ronan had told her he could fix her, but she had to lie down. The pain was making her loopy.

Ronan handled her left foot gently, getting it as straight as he could. He then gripped the hem of her pant leg and tore it in half, all the way up to her thigh.

She jolted at that, trying to sit up. "Hey!" Loopy she may be, but she wasn't going down without a fight.

He pushed her back down. "Lie still. If you move too much I could set your bones wrong. They'd heal crooked and you wouldn't be able to walk normally again."

That made her stop struggling. She didn't want to be hobbled anymore. It made her feel weak and vulnerable.

"Take in a deep breath."

She did, just as he wrapped his hands around her ankle and pressed down.

Pure dark agony sang up her leg. She gritted her teeth and bit down on her tongue. Blood filled her mouth, but it at least made her think about something other than the pain searing her foot.

Sweat dampened her forehead. She felt faint, light-headed. She was in fear of passing out any second. Then the pain receded a little. Just enough that she could put together some coherent thoughts.

She glanced down her body to her feet. She could see a faint blue glow around her left ankle. It emitted from Ronan's hands as he held her still, pressing tight against her bones. His eyes were closed, and she could see the muscles at his jawline flexing. His face was sweat slicked, and she wondered if he, too, was in pain. It appeared that he was.

Finally, after what felt like an eternity, the pain stopped. Instead, a warm floating feeling settled into her bones and muscles. It was as if she was suspended on her back in a sea of warm water.

Ronan let her ankle go and stood up, looking

down at her. His brow was still creased but he didn't have that pained look in his eyes.

She smiled up at him. She couldn't help it; she felt giddy. "Wow. You're good."

"Your bone is fused back together. I also infused you with a kick of endorphins. That's what you're feeling right now."

"I like it." She reached up to him and grabbed his hand. But his skin seared her and she snatched back her hand. "Ow. You burned me."

Ronan rubbed the palms of his hands on his pants. "Part of the process, I'm afraid. Healing burns my hands."

"Are you in pain?"

He shrugged. "Nothing I can't handle."

"You should shoot yourself up with those endorphins."

"Doesn't work like that." He continued to rub his hands on his legs, looking down at them with a forlorn look on his face. A look of loss, maybe.

She liked looking at him. He was an attractive man, with that dark tousled hair and those intense eyes. He had strong facial features and a full mouth. She remembered how those lips had felt on her skin. And she longed to feel them again. Maybe she could erase the pain from his eyes.

She slid over on the mattress and patted it beside her. "There's room for two. You need some sleep, as well."

He considered her. "That's the endorphins talking."

"I don't care." She grabbed his hand again, this time holding on tight despite the burning sensation. She tugged him to the bed.

He knelt one knee on the mattress, then settled his full weight down beside her. He stretched out on his side, his body barely brushing against hers. But she could still feel the heat of him covering her.

She turned onto her side to look at him. To really look at him. She traced one finger along his jawline to his mouth. He opened his lips slightly as she ran her fingertip over them. "You're really quite beautiful."

He reached up and stilled her hand on his mouth to softly kiss her fingertips. "So are you."

"You know, I really don't want to like you."

"I know." He smiled and kissed her fingers again. "I don't want to like you, either."

"Even with your demon blood, you're a better man than most I've known."

"And for a hunter, you're a damn fine woman."

She laughed at that, then wrapped her hand around his neck and pulled him close. She covered his mouth with hers and kissed him hard.

At first he hesitated a little, but his resolve soon broke and he was fisting his hands in her hair and tilting her head to deepen the kiss. Lips touching, tongues stroking, teeth nibbling. It was a long, hard, wet kiss that made her stomach clench and her thighs tingle with anticipation.

Ronan broke the kiss and stared into her eyes. He traced his fingers down her cheek to her neck and back. "We don't have to, you know. I could just hold you."

She snorted. "Oh, no, we have to."

"I don't want to hurt you."

"I'm feeling no pain right now."

He shook his head. "It's not the right time."

She kissed his protests away, and then nibbled on his earlobe. "It's the perfect time. I need you, Ronan. I need to forget everything for a while. Don't make me beg."

He stilled his fingers on her face, then pulled her close to press his lips to hers. He shoved his other arm under her to cradle her body next to his. She could feel the thumping of his heart. It was as fast and fierce as her own.

She moved her hand down to the hem of his T-shirt, and yanked it up. Ronan sat up briefly to pull the cotton over his head. When he lay beside her again, she ran her hand over his chest, playing her fingers over the thin line of dark hair that lined his sternum down to his pants.

He rubbed his hand over her arm to the edge of her shirt. His hand snuck up under the fabric to capture one breast in his palm. He pulled at the cotton cup of her bra to find her nipple already hard and throbbing for his touch. He pinched and pulled on her until she was moaning.

"Oh, your hand is still hot."

"Does it hurt?"

She shook her head. "God, no. Feels fantastic."

Ivy's hand roamed down his chest to the button of his pants. She made quick work of it and unzipped him. His erection strained against the cotton of his black briefs. She covered him with her hand and massaged him through the fabric.

Growling low in his throat, Ronan sat her up and stripped off her shirt in one pull. He nestled her down again beside him; his head bent low to her breasts. Tugging at her bra, he quickly sucked in one nipple, rolling it between tongue and teeth, and then lavished equal attention on the other.

His hand was edging down to her pants. "I don't want to upset your ankle by taking off your pants."

"Just tear them off. You already halfway did anyway."

"True." He grinned, and then with one impressive pull he ripped the rest of her pants away, tugging the torn material out from under her and tossing it onto the floor, leaving her in just her panties. "There. Perfect."

She half moaned, half laughed as he yanked on her cotton panties to pull them down over her hips. Then his fingers, still hot and sweaty, were buried between her legs, stroking her gently, and she lost all thought and reason.

Ronan had to bite down on his lip to stop from tearing into her. The feel of her hot slick lust on his hand was enough to leave him feeling hard, hot, and desperate to take her until she screamed his name.

Desire clawed at him as he nuzzled her breasts. He bit down on a nipple while plunging his fingers into her core. She cried out as he stroked her fast. He wanted to watch her face when she came. He wanted to see the ecstasy in her eyes. Ecstasy that he gave her.

His fingers pumped harder and faster until her breath came in short pants. He sucked on her nipples, hard, nipping at her skin every so often. He alternated between plunging into her and flicking his fingers over her clit. He could feel the muscles in her body clench.

She squeezed her eyes shut as he pinched her sensitive nub then stroked her firmly again. Back and forth he went. Rubbing, flicking and pumping. Until her hand tightened on his cock and he knew she was going over the edge.

And just as she came, Ronan tugged down his briefs, pulled her leg up over his hip and plunged his cock into her in one swift, powerful thrust.

Her eyes flashed open and she cried out. "Ronan!"

Gripping her behind with his hand, he drove into her again and again. He pumped and thrust until his whole body was wet with sweat. Until the muscles in his legs and arms vibrated with strain.

She was panting and mewling, her hands everywhere on him, pulling and tearing and holding on. He gritted his teeth and pulled her down to him as he thrust up hard with his hips. He buried himself deep inside her. Her flesh contracted around him, squeezing him tight.

Then, in a flash of light and heat and delicious agony, he came.

For five minutes, neither one of them moved. It was as if they were frozen in time, fused together like some complicated marble statue.

Ronan opened his eyes and studied her face. Her eyes were still closed and she was almost smiling. It was sexy the way her lips twitched up at the side. She must've sensed he was looking at her because the smile widened.

"I'd say I've completely forgotten about my ankle."

"Well, good. My work here is done, then."

Ivy opened her eyes and met his gaze. "I'd say that you earned some overtime pay."

"Is that right?"

"Yup." She snuggled closer to him and pressed her lips to his neck. She traced her fingers up and down the line of his sternum. "Mmm, you smell like perfection."

He chuckled at that. "I think you're drugged from sex."

"You think right." She closed her eyes and nuzzled her face into the crook of his neck and shoulder. Her hand curled up to rest on his chest.

He pulled her tight, his other hand resting on the rise of her hip. He played it gently back and forth along her smooth, pale skin.

She sighed. The cadence of her breathing slowed and he sensed the exact moment when she fell asleep. With his chin resting on her head, he smiled, and then closed his eyes, allowing himself to drift off. And just before he was asleep, Ronan thought how perfectly they fit together.

Chapter 17

Ivy jolted awake. Rubbing at her eyes, she slowly sat up. Did something wake her? Had she heard a strange noise? She glanced up and saw a fat brown squirrel at the window. Its thick bushy tail thwacked against the glass as it busily collected food.

A bit confused about where she was, she looked around the small room. Her gaze landed on Ronan sleeping next to her on the bed. He was naked, a sheet lightly drawn over his hip. She drank in his naked form. He was definitely a looker. No doubt about it.

She shook her head. But what the hell was she doing having sex with him again? Hadn't she learned the first time? No good could come of their...

Whatever it was. It would only get in the way. And once they found Quinn and Ronan took the key, or tried to, what would they have in common anymore?

She rubbed at her face again, then swung her legs off the bed. She set her feet down on the floor and tested her left ankle. It was sore, but looking down at it, no one would ever be able to tell that the bone had snapped and ruptured her skin. The flesh around her ankle was bruised dark purple, but there were no lacerations. No puncture wound. She glanced over her shoulder at Ronan. He was truly gifted with the power to heal within his demon blood. Go figure.

A cool breeze blew over her skin, bringing attention to the fact that she was naked. Everything had ended up coming off during their hot sex session. She stood, wobbled a bit then went to search for her bag for a pair of pants.

Once she was dressed in khakis and a T-shirt, she went to see about finding them some food. They both needed the energy. Especially after the sexual bout they'd had. It had been intense and her thighs and belly still clenched in remembrance. Her orgasm had been fierce and not something she could easily erase from her mind.

With one last glance at Ronan's sleeping form, she silently exited the room. She stole across the hall and into the kitchen, careful not to make any noise in case someone had come home without their knowledge. Once in the kitchen, Ivy glanced out the window to the drive. There were no vehicles parked on the dirt path. She breathed a sigh of relief and began searching the cupboards and pantry for something edible.

After a thorough search, she dumped a can of mushroom soup into a saucepan and brought it to a boil on the stove. She also found some crackers to go with it. As she stirred the soup, she thought about their next step. The first thing was to find a vehicle and get back on the road. Getting to Quinn was even more important than before. Because someone obviously didn't want that to happen. This was the second attempt on her life. Well, both their lives.

She'd thought the first attempt, at her house, had been the demon Sallos's doing, but now she wasn't so sure. What if someone else wanted to stop her from finding Quinn? It obviously wasn't the Crimson Hall Cabal. No, they wanted her to get to Quinn so Ronan could take the key for them. So, if not them, then who?

"Smells good."

Ivy swung around to see Ronan leaning casually in the kitchen doorway. He'd slipped on a pair of pants, but forwent a shirt. And she couldn't stop herself from gobbling up his hard pecs, flat stomach and the dark line of hair that arrowed down to the waistband of his pants. Her fingers itched as she remembered tracing a seductive trail down that path.

"It's mushroom. All I could find. There was tomato but I hate tomato."

"Yeah, me, too." He came all the way into the kitchen and sat at the little two-seater table.

Ivy turned off the stove, and then poured the soup into two big bowls. She set the bowls down on the table along with spoons and the box of crackers.

She expected him to pick up his spoon and start eating, but instead he stared at her expectantly. She stared back, not sure what he wanted her to say. It wasn't like she'd had a lot of experience in morning afters. She usually didn't sleep with men. She'd had sex, but she'd usually kick them out afterward. It was interesting that sleeping beside Ronan had been more intimate than any of her prior sexual escapades.

After another minute, Ronan sighed, then picked up the spoon and began to ladle the soup into his mouth. He grabbed a couple of crackers, crushed them into the soup and continued to eat.

She followed suit, until a few minutes later they both had empty bowls.

He wiped at his mouth with the back of his hand. "So I figure we need a vehicle."

"I was just thinking that."

"There's a small barn in the back. I'll check it to see if there's anything that's useful."

She nodded. "We need to get back on the road as soon as possible. That second attack tells me that we are on the right track to Quinn."

"I know." He pushed back his chair and stood. He left the kitchen and returned to the den, she assumed to put on a shirt and his boots. After another minute, she heard the back door open and close.

This gave her time to go back into the den, get her boots and gear—and her mind—back together. Nothing was going to get accomplished with her fantasizing about Ronan's body and remembering how it felt as he filled her tight. She had to put her mind where it needed to be: on finding Quinn. Nothing else was important. No matter how much her body told her otherwise.

Ronan marched across the back lawn to the barnlike building. Anger made the muscles along his jawline jump. He supposed he shouldn't have expected anything other than the cool reception she'd given him. It wasn't like she was going to prance across the kitchen floor and fling her arms around him to kiss him. It was just that he thought maybe something had changed last night, was hoping that something had shifted between them.

He didn't want it to be just sex between them. He wanted more from her.

But wanting more from the ice-queen demon hunter was a lesson in futility. It wasn't going to happen. And he had to get that through his head. He was a means to an end for Ivy. And that was all he was ever going to be.

The door to the barn opened easily and he stepped in. It smelled of mildew and old hay but also had the unmistakable odor of motor oil. He smiled when he saw the vehicle barely visible in the shadows. He hoped it would run.

He approached the car, a two-door Ford T-Bird, running his hand along the old hood. The windows were cranked open and he peered inside at the dark leather interior. He smiled again. He really liked old cars. This one was a classic and it looked like the owner took real good care of it.

"Is it drivable?"

Ronan swung around to see Ivy standing in the open doorway. "Looks to be in good condition."

"Can you hot-wire this thing?"

He nodded. "Oh, yeah, no problem. It's a lot

easier to hot-wire old cars compared to new ones. All I need is a screwdriver."

She moved along one of the workbenches, searching the surface for tools. She found what he needed, picked it up and handed it to him. Their fingers brushed as he took it. There was an electric jolt between them.

Ronan's eyes came up and locked on hers. "Ivy, maybe we should—"

"No need to talk about it." She went to leave, but he grabbed her arm and pulled her back.

"Last night was more than just sex."

She didn't deny it, just stared into his eyes.

"I think we should talk about it."

She shrugged. "Why? What does it matter? Does it change our plans?"

"No."

"Then why can't we just leave it be?"

"Because it matters." He tugged her closer to him. "You matter. I want you to know that in case, you know, anything happens."

"Fine. I know it. Thank you."

He wanted to shake her. She was so exasperating. He leaned down and covered her mouth with his. He kissed her hard, snaking his tongue between her lips, tasting her, possessing her.

She moaned into him, fisting her hands into his shirt. She gave just as good as he did. Trading stroke for stroke, nibble for nibble. They kissed until they were both breathless.

Ronan pulled away and rested his forehead against hers. "Don't you have anything to say to me?"

She was silent for a moment, but he could tell she was thinking, considering her next words. She sighed, and then said, "Fine. You matter to me, too. There, are you happy now?"

He pulled back and smiled, then chucked her chin. "Yup."

She shook her head at him. "Great. Now get this car running and I'll go get our gear. I want to be out of here in the next ten minutes."

He saluted her. "Yes, sir."

She turned on her heel to leave, but he saw her grin before she exited the barn.

Chapter 18

True to Ivy's command, they were back on the road within ten minutes. Ronan had easily hot-wired the old T-Bird and they were cruising down the main road in the baby-blue car. Ronan was grinning the whole time, clearly enjoying the fact that he was driving the classic car.

She couldn't care less. It was a vehicle and it would get them from point A to point B. Point B being, hopefully, where Quinn was located. She almost felt frantic now that she was so close. This was the best lead she'd had on his location in the past three years. Everything else had been rumors or mistaken identity.

She was still trying to decide the first thing

she was going to do when she saw Quinn again. Either hug him or punch him in his pointy chin. Right now she was still fifty-one, forty-nine, the former being the punch.

If only it was that easy with another man.

She glanced briefly at Ronan. He'd made her admit something she wasn't quite ready to cop to. But his kiss had been fierce and it had pulled at something inside her. It had been more than a lusty punch in the gut; it had tugged at her heart. Just a little, mind you. But it was enough that she couldn't ignore it.

And the feeling wasn't going to go away anytime soon. Especially since she was still saddled with the cambion for another few days at least. Once they found Quinn, then what? Would he go his own way? She hoped so. Then she could shake him from her psyche.

Until then, he was firmly planted there. It was an inconvenient truth, but she had to deal with it.

After another couple of hours, they drove through Salem, stopping for lunch and much-needed coffee. They grabbed a couple of burgers and got back onto the highway. Another few hours and they would hit Washington, then the small town of Sumner, where supposedly her brother was holed up.

It seemed like a really odd place for him to be.

But knowing Quinn, he had his reasons. Strange they might be, but he had them. He was always like that. Doing things unconventionally, but when he explained why, it would all make perfect sense.

Ivy missed him a lot. He'd always been her strength and her direction. Living without his leadership had been hard. But she'd done it. Thrived even. Maybe that had been his whole point.

"What are you thinking about?"

She turned and looked at Ronan.

"Your brow is creased. Looks like you're thinking about killing someone."

"Quinn. When I see him."

He chuckled. "Ah. I thought maybe it was me."

"Well, not right now." She smirked. "Who's going to drive this junker?"

"Good point."

For the next few hours, they didn't speak, which Ivy appreciated. The silence was surprisingly comfortable. As if they'd known each other for years instead of days. That was just another thing she liked about him. He knew when she needed the quiet. When she needed to be left to her thoughts.

It was late afternoon when they drove into Washington state. Only three more hours before they hit the town of Sumner. Ivy wasn't sure what she expected when they arrived. Would Quinn still be there, or would he have moved on? For some reason she sensed the former. That he was still there. The closer they got, the more on edge she felt. Something was definitely going on in the small town of Sumner.

She'd looked up the place on the internet before they left. There was nothing remarkable about the town. It was like any other sleepy picturesque American town. The council met every Wednesday night, and the Thanksgiving parade promised a giant turkey and more pumpkin pie than the average person could eat. There was nothing supernatural about the place.

After another hour, Ivy's head started to pound. She'd had plenty of headaches before, some self-induced, but this one was different. It came on like gangbusters and wouldn't relent. It was as if some tiny person with a chisel and a hammer had crouched up inside her skull and was chipping away at her brain.

She brought a hand up to her temples and started to rub them hard, wincing the whole time.

"What's wrong?"

"My head hurts."

Frowning, he reached over the seat and touched her shoulder. "Did it just come on?"

She nodded, her tongue too thick to talk.

"I'm pulling over." He swerved to the shoulder

and came to a stop. Once parked, he turned toward her. "Let me see."

She turned to him. He pushed her hands away from her temples and wrapped both his hands around her head, his fingers splayed wide. She could feel the pressure of his fingers on her skull and she wanted to pry them off, but she knew he was trying to take the pain away. After a few more minutes, the screaming agony in her head abated. She sighed and felt herself go lax. Ronan removed his hands from her head and set them on her shoulders.

She looked him in the eyes. "I have a feeling this means something."

He nodded. "I can feel it in my head, too. It doesn't hurt me as much, though."

"What does it mean?"

"It means we're going to be walking into a shit storm."

"Demons?"

He nodded again. "I fear there's more going on in Sumner than just Quinn hiding away."

"How long until we get there?"

"Two hours max."

"I suggest we arm ourselves, then, before we hit town."

"Agreed."

Twenty minutes later, they both had their knives

strapped to their bodies with varying harnesses. Ronan had his shotgun laid across his lap, loaded with blessed rock salt and silver shots. Ivy outfitted herself with several holy-water ampuls and a liquid-silver spray. She'd put it together like a can of mace. Effectively, it was used in the same way. A silver shot to a demon's eyes was enough to blind.

The silence was palpable as they drove down the highway toward town. Ivy could feel Ronan's edginess as well as her own. His gaze darted everywhere at once, looking for something, anything to be out of place.

She just kept her eyes on the road ahead. In the distance, large rolling black clouds gathered. It looked like they were waiting for them to drive right into their dark folds. They had that ominous quality reserved for black magic and demons.

Usually she wasn't afraid when she went on a hunt. It was a job, a job she was good at and had trained for, for many years. Sometimes it was a cakewalk to take out the hellspawn. This all felt different. Something major was happening. And she wasn't confident that she was prepared enough to handle it.

For the next hour and a half, Ronan drove in silence, his gaze fierce and alert. She glanced out the side window every now and then, but for the most part watched the road in front of them. One thing she did notice was there was virtually no traffic on the highway. No cars in front of them, nothing behind them and no vehicles in the opposite lanes. Which was odd even for an untraveled highway.

As they took the ramp off I-5 and closed in on the town, evidence to confirm her paranoia started to show. At the sign welcoming them to Sumner, there were two cars in the ditch, the doors flung open but no sign of the occupants. Ronan slowed a little as Ivy peered into the empty vehicles.

"Do you see anything?" he asked.

She shook her head. "Nothing."

They continued on, driving slowly down the street that headed into the main town square. They passed a few old houses along the way, cars in drives, but no one in the yards. That didn't necessarily mean anything. Dark clouds did swirl overhead threateningly. Residents might be hunkering down inside waiting for the storm to pass.

But Ivy had a feeling this storm wasn't going to move on anytime soon.

After another five minutes, Ronan drove the car into downtown Sumner. But it was like no downtown she'd ever seen. There were cars parked here and there, haphazardly, clearly not obeying any of the parking laws. One SUV was overturned on its side, all its windows bashed in.

Some of the storefront windows were also smashed in. Parts of the sidewalks were littered with broken glass. And if her eyes didn't deceive her, she spotted blood splatters here and there on the cement and on the brick store walls.

But as they made a pass down the main street, they didn't spy one person on the street, in their cars, or in the open store doors. It looked like a ghost town. Most recently deceased.

"Looks like a war zone," Ronan muttered as they turned onto another street and off the main drag.

"Yeah, but a war between who?"

And that's when a large something smashed on top of their car, denting in the roof.

Chapter 19

Ronan lost control of the steering wheel and veered off to the right, bumping up onto the curb and sidewalk. "Jesus! What was that?"

That answer came when a body rolled down the windshield and over the hood to land in a heap in front of the car.

He glanced at Ivy, who had two knives unsheathed and was staring out the front window. "Do you think he was thrown or did he jump?" she asked.

"I don't know. I don't think we should stick around to find out." He put the car in Reverse and backed up off the curb and onto the street.

The body that had "fallen" onto the roof of their

car struggled to his feet. He looked like an average guy, average height and weight, wearing a flannel shirt, jeans and runners. But when he turned toward the car and grinned at them, blood dripping down his chin from what looked like a busted nose and some missing teeth, Ronan knew there wasn't anything average about this guy.

"Welcome to Sumner, bitches!" The guy lurched ahead, reaching for the car.

"Jesus, the bastard's possessed," Ivy hissed. "I wonder how many others are, as well."

Ronan glanced in his rearview mirror and saw three more people, two men and a young woman, coming up on their rear, grinning like fools. "I'm going to guess and say a bunch." He shot it into Drive and stepped on the gas. "Hang on."

He raced down the street, then took another left to avoid going back down the main drag. As they zipped down the road, veering around two more abandoned vehicles in the middle of the street, Ronan noticed another car following behind.

"We've got company."

Ivy glanced over her shoulder and through the back window. "He's gaining on us."

"I can see that."

He cranked the wheel to the left, jumped the curb and drove half on, half off the sidewalk to avoid another car sitting in the street. Coming up on the next corner, he took it at top speed, skidding to the side, but he kept in control. A glance in the rearview mirror showed the other vehicle slagging off.

He was about to smile when in his periphery he spied a truck coming at them from the side. "Hang on!" he yelled just as the truck slammed hard into the passenger side, barely missing the door.

The impact sent them into a spin. Ronan could barely steer as the car careened off the road and slammed into a light post, crushing the front end like an accordion. He knocked his forehead against the steering wheel. Thankfully he'd been wearing a seat belt or else he would've gone through the windshield.

He turned to his side to check on Ivy. She, too, had hit her head on the dashboard, but didn't fare as well. She had a big gash above her right eye. Blood dribbled down her face, obscuring her vision. She wiped at it with the back of her hand.

He reached over and touched her shoulder. "Are you—" His heart slammed in his chest. "Out of the car! Out! Now!" He pushed the release on her seat belt and, grabbing her hand, yanked her across the seat. He pushed open his door and slid out, pulling her with him.

They both tumbled to the ground. But Ronan scrambled up, tugged his shotgun out of the car, and yanked Ivy to her feet. By now, she'd totally seen the truck roaring toward their smashed car and was already running full speed away from the scene.

He caught up with her just as she jumped over a small white fence around some person's front yard. They plowed across the green grass toward a side fence. Without stopping, Ronan kicked the wooden gate off its hinges and they raced alongside the bungalow and into the backyard. Thankfully there was no guard dog on duty.

They crossed the yard to the back fence, which butted up to another yard. It was a six-foot wooden structure and not easily jumped. When Ronan got to it, he bent down and cupped his hands for Ivy. She stepped up into them, grabbed hold of the top and hefted herself over. Once she landed, he vaulted it in one leap.

She sniffed at him. "Must be nice."

"It doesn't hurt, that's for sure."

"Now where?"

"We can't stop here. I suspect they'll be looking for us." He glanced to the side and down the row of houses. "I say we jump a couple more fences that way, then into a house. We need a minute to figure this out."

"Let's not take too long, okay?"

After they jumped three more fences, they

found a house with an unlocked sliding-glass balcony door. They entered the house. No one was at home. But it looked like it had been vacated in a hurry. There were half-eaten meals on the table, and the TV was on in the living room. It appeared that the occupants had either jumped ship or been taken out.

Ivy opened the refrigerator and found a couple of bottles of water. She tossed one to Ronan and uncapped the other, taking some greedy gulps. She finished half the bottle, then capped it again.

"So what are we dealing with? An entire possessed town?"

He drank some water, and then shrugged. "I don't know. I've never seen anything like this. Never heard of anything like this, either." He neared her, and grabbing a dish towel, he splashed it with some water and dabbed at the cut on her forehead.

It wasn't bleeding freely anymore, which was good. He wiped at it and saw that it was sealing up. For good measure he pressed his thumb to it to help it along. After a solid minute he dropped his hand and took a step back.

She nodded to him. "Thanks."

"You're welcome." He wanted to pull her to him and kiss her, or at least hold her close. They'd nearly been hurt badly. He wouldn't be able to stand it if she had been. His healing came with limits. He wasn't able to mend everything. Serious wounds were beyond his scope. If she'd been crushed in the car, he doubted if he would have been able to save her.

He didn't want to think about it. It hurt too much to consider it. So he made his way into the living room to peer out the front window and assess their situation. Crouching, he pushed aside one part of the sunny-yellow drape and peered out to the street.

A car rolled by, slowly making its way down the street. He imagined the occupant was looking for them. Then he saw three people walking down the sidewalk. It was the same three people he'd seen earlier, coming up behind their car. He ducked down as they passed the house.

Ivy crawled to where he was situated. "What did you see?"

"The three that passed were demons."

"Are you sure?"

He nodded. "Positive. They weren't hiding their red eyes."

"So we have a bunch of demons and possessed townspeople."

"Looks like it."

"Where's the resistance? I saw some bullet

holes along the main street and some blood. There have to be people here fighting against them."

"Your brother among them?"

She nodded. "Let's hope so."

"Well, I'm going to go out on a limb here and say that if there is a resistance, they definitely would've been alerted to our presence. We did make a kind of splashy entrance."

Smiling, Ivy said, "Yeah, I'd say."

"So the best way for them to find us is out on the street, not hiding in this house."

"I hate sneaking around anyway. It's not my style."

He looked her over, taking in everything about her, and grinned. "No, it certainly isn't."

"I think our best bet would be back out on Main Street."

"Agreed." He glanced out the window again. "We're only a block away. We can sprint across the street and through that side fence." He pointed to a spot two doors down. "I imagine there'll be an alleyway separating the houses and the back of the main stores."

"Okay." She unsheathed two of her longest, deadliest blades. "I'm good for close work."

Ronan pumped a round into his shotgun. "I got you covered."

"Good. Then let's not waste time by talking."

She was about to open the front door when he grabbed her arm to stop her. He leaned down and kissed her. He had to. He couldn't go into whatever it was they were going into without having felt her lips on his once more.

When they broke apart, she licked her lips. "Don't look at me like we're not going to get through this. Because we are. I won't let anything happen to you. Don't worry."

He laughed at that. "Okay, I won't."

She gave him her most winning smile, and then opened the front door. On a count of three, they ran out onto the street and hopefully not to their doom.

They crossed the street with little problem and went into the backyard of the house two down from their hiding spot. The back fence was another tall one, and he'd been right about it butting up against an alley.

Before they jumped it, Ronan peered through the slats. He looked down one way, then the other. So far, the coast was clear. "Looks good." He bent over and gave Ivy a hand up. Once she was on top of the fence, she swung her legs over and jumped down.

"Clear," she said, as she waited for him.

He vaulted up on top of the fence and perched

there for only a second. But it was enough for a bullet to find him and pierce through his shoulder.

The impact sent him spiraling off the fence. He landed on his side on the gravel. Ivy was on him in seconds, pulling him up, but mindful of his bloodied arm.

"Shit. You've been shot."

"It's fine. I'll live. Let's get out of here."

Together, they scrambled out of the alley, down another, between two stores and out onto Main Street. Here there were more people milling about. Ronan didn't know if they were demons or the possessed. He couldn't tell from this distance. And as far as he could discern, he and Ivy hadn't been spotted yet.

He motioned toward one burned car. "Over there. We can hunker down behind it."

They ran to the car and crouched behind the back bumper. Ivy pulled at his shirt. "Let me see."

Ronan rolled up his sleeve over his shoulder. Blood ran down from the wound. He prodded it with his finger. "It's not bad." He searched behind and found the exit hole. "It went through."

"We need to patch you up." She reached into the pack she had strapped to her belt. She unzipped it and came away with some alcohol wipes and some gauze pads. She ripped open the wipe package. "It's going to sting."

"Can't hurt more than it already does."

"Don't be a baby." She wiped it across the open wound.

Ronan nearly shot to his feet. The pain was sharp and stinging. It almost brought tears to his eyes. After she finished, she pressed the hole with three gauze pads and secured them with tape. When she was done, she rolled down his shirt-sleeve.

He tested the tape job by rolling his shoulder. "Not bad."

She shrugged. "You're not the only one that can heal."

He lifted up his shotgun again and peered around the car. The people that had been on the street were now gone. He scanned the storefronts and the rooftops. Nothing. He didn't like the feeling that crept over him.

"I think we may have a problem."

The metal barrel nudging the back of his head confirmed that statement.

"What are you doing out here making all this noise?" the male gunman asked.

"Trying to get your attention," Ivy answered.

Ronan pictured another gunman pointing a weapon at Ivy. There was no way this one guy would still be standing if there hadn't been.

"Yeah, well, you definitely got it now," the gunman answered.

"They're demons, Bill," the other gunman said. "Let's take them out and get out of here."

Ronan heard a round going into a chamber.

"Wait," Ivy growled. "My name is Ivy Strom and I'm here looking for my brother, Quinn Strom. Do you know him?"

There was an audible sigh from one of the two men, and then Ronan heard a safety going on. Obviously they'd heard of Quinn Strom.

"You better be who you say you are, or you're going to die, nice and slow."

Chapter 20

The two human gunmen blindfolded Ivy and Ronan, stuffed them into the back of a car and drove them to their camp. Ivy wondered if that was where Quinn was. She imagined if there was a leader running this show it would definitely be him. That's why she had used his name as a stalling method. It had obviously worked like a charm.

After about a ten-minute drive, a long time for such a small town, the vehicle came to a stop. She figured they were then just outside the town limits. The car doors opened and they were pulled out and pushed down a path of some sort, up four stairs and through a door. Ivy heard it shut behind them. Then they were ushered—she could sense

Ronan with her still—across a floor and down a set of stairs to a basement, she assumed. Once there, they were shoved into hard wooden chairs and their blindfolds were tugged off.

She was right; they were in a basement of some older house, surrounded by about ten men and women, all with weapons trained on her and Ronan. She sniffed. Mildew, sweat and fear tainted the air. It was an old house filled with frightened people. She wondered how long they'd been holed up like this. Then she looked down and saw her chair was smack dab in the middle of a devil's trap. She glanced over at Ronan and saw the same thing.

He lifted an eyebrow and a shoulder in response.

Another man stepped forward. He looked to be around thirty—dirty, sweaty and tired. There was a fresh bandage around his hand. "Who are you? And what are you doing in Sumner?"

"I'll only talk to the man in charge," Ivy said, looking around at the faces glaring at them.

"I am in charge," he retorted with a sniff.

She shook her head. "No, you're not. Quinn Strom is here somewhere. This totally looks like his operation."

"Perceptive, as always, I see."

The deep masculine voice came from behind her but she would know it anywhere. She sighed, then gave a little chuckle. "Enough to know that you haven't had a bath in, say, over a week."

Quinn came around her chair, stepping into her view. He looked the same. His hair was a little longer, flecked with a little gray at the sides. Dark stubble lined his pointy jaw. She wanted to punch that jaw.

"Hello, sis."

"Quinn." She gestured to the people with guns pointing at her. "Is this how you treat the last of your family?"

"When they could be possessed by demons, sure is." He glanced at Ronan. And Ivy could see his amulet flare to life. Instantly, he drew his own weapon, cocked it.

"Don't!" she yelled. "Don't splatter him all over the place."

Quinn looked at her from the corner of his eye. "Why, is he your demon lover?"

She saw Ronan bristle at that.

"He's not full-blooded. He's a cambion. Turned against his will." She reached out a hand. "Just give us holy water to drink, jerk, so we can prove who we are and be done with this bullshit."

Quinn nodded to the woman on his right. She rushed over and handed an open bottle of water to Ivy. She snatched it from the woman's hand, tipped it and chugged half the bottle. She was definitely thirsty, and holy water or not, it hit the spot. After she wiped her mouth with the back of her hand, she handed it back to the woman.

"There. You see. I'm not possessed."

Quinn didn't say anything, just nodded at the woman again. When she approached Ronan she was much more cautious. Afraid looking, even. Her hand shook as she handed it to him.

Ronan took the bottle, and after giving a cheers to Quinn, he chugged down the rest. He burped, wiped his mouth and tossed the bottle onto the floor. "Satisfied, big guy?"

"No, but I guess it proves you aren't a demon. Doesn't mean I can trust you."

"He's with me, so you can trust him," Ivy said.

Quinn nodded to his men, who all lowered their weapons. He then turned to look at Ivy. "Nice to see you, Ivy."

She jumped to her feet, crossed the room and wrapped her arms around him. He hugged her back, tight. The familiar scent of him filled her nose and she sighed again.

When they broke apart, she took a step back, and fisting her hand, she punched him in the jaw. He stumbled back and, rubbing his face, he laughed. "Not bad. You've gotten stronger."

"You're an asshole."

Once he recovered, he eyed her sharply. "Why are you here? How did you find me?"

"I came to bring you home, jackass."

He glanced at Ronan. "So are you going to enlighten me on who this guy is and why you are running around with a cambion?"

"It's a long story and frankly doesn't matter. The fact is, I've been looking for you for the past three years and now I've found you."

Quinn shook his head. "Yeah. I didn't think you would."

"You're my brother, idiot. Of course I'm going to try to find you."

"Didn't you get my note?"

"Oh, you mean the one that said 'Don't try and find me'?" She snorted. "I saw it and tossed it away. Did you really think I would listen?"

He chuckled. "I suppose I should've known better."

"Yeah, duh."

Quinn's gaze roamed over Ronan again. And he shook his head. "I'm sorry. I just have a real hard time accepting that you are running with this guy. I thought you hated demons like the rest of us."

Ivy glanced over her shoulder at Ronan. He was leaning back in his chair, all casual-like. But she knew he was primed and ready to act at a nanosecond's notice. He'd defend himself vigorously if attacked. She really didn't want to be mopping up both his and her brother's blood.

"I do hate demons. But Ronan isn't one. So get that through your thick skull."

"I'm just remembering the last time you brought a guy home, he turned out to be a demon."

She glared at him. "Oh, grow up, Quinn. I was sixteen then."

"What was his name again?"

"Nick," she bit out between clenched teeth. "And you solved the problem, Quinn, you saw right through him and splattered him into a billion pieces in front of me. So what, that makes you a big hero, huh?"

She hated remembering that night. It was a turning point for her. The night she'd promised herself never to get involved with another guy. They could hurt you in more ways than one if they got too close. She'd learned that in all kinds of hard ways that night.

Just one more reason why building a relationship with Ronan was impossible. In the back of her mind, she'd always be afraid that Quinn would splatter him all over the room just as he did to her last serious boyfriend who turned out to be a demon.

"Besides, I'm not dating Ronan. He's my busi-

ness partner. It's a completely different set of circumstances."

She could see Ronan tense in his chair, but she
didn't want to face him. Not yet. Not now. She had
to make sure her stupid brother didn't kill him or
something equally as inane.

Quinn laughed, then put his hands up. "Okay,
okay. You don't have to get nasty."

"Oh, you haven't seen nasty. I've taken nasty
to a whole new level during the past three years."

Quinn lost his indignant smile, and then ran a
hand over his face. He looked tired, she thought.
Worn out. Again she wondered how long they'd
been hunkered down in this fight.

"Yeah, well, I guess a lot has changed, hasn't
it?"

She nodded. "Yup." But the fight had drained
out of her. She no longer wanted to beat the crap
out of him for leaving her. Well, maybe still a little. She just wanted to know if he was all right,
and how she could help him.

"Can I get up now?" Ronan asked.

Quinn nodded. "I guess, but I still don't trust
you, so don't be doing anything stupid."

Ronan stood. "Fair enough." He came up along
Ivy's side. She wanted to lean into him, but with
her brother still eyeing Ronan and her, she re-
frained and kept her feet in place.

"So what the hell is going on around here?" she asked. "Looks like a war zone out there."

"It is," Quinn answered.

"When did this all happen?"

He sighed, and then rested a hip up against a wood table along one wall. "About three days ago."

Ivy flinched at that and glanced at Ronan. Three days ago she had just met Ronan in the dark back alley. The cambion didn't meet her gaze; he kept his eyes on Quinn.

"How did it start?"

"Some people started going bat-shit crazy." Quinn nodded toward the woman that had given them the water. "Started with Julie's husband. He drove his truck into the police station and shot Sheriff Newman. Deputy Bradford shot and killed him." He sighed again. "Julie came to me about it, and I went and looked at the body in the morgue. Saw evidence of possession."

Julie started to cry. One of the other men hugged her close and patted her on the back.

"It escalated in a hurry."

"We saw three demons earlier," Ronan said.

Quinn nodded. "I'd say there are at least ten in town. Maybe more."

"Why here?" Ivy asked, but she had a feeling she already knew the answer and was looking at it in his familiar face.

He shook his head. "I'm not sure."

"Okay, I'll make it easy for you," she said. "Why are you here? What made you come to this town of all places?"

He didn't answer at first, but shuffled his shoe on the floor. "I made a promise to Dad."

"What?" That was the last thing Ivy expected to hear. "What promise?"

"That I would take care of things when he was gone."

"Yeah, so? What needed to be taken care of here?"

Another woman stepped forward. She was older, in her fifties for sure, with a tanned face. Her dark hair was lined with gray and pulled back into a severe ponytail. "Me."

Ivy swung around toward her. "And who are you?"

Quinn looked at them both sheepishly. "Ivy, this is Gloria. Gloria was Dad's…"

"Mistress," Ivy finished for him. "Yeah, I get it. And?"

Gloria's eyes widened with surprise, and maybe hurt, but Ivy didn't care. She didn't have time to coddle anyone. They were all grown-ups, weren't they?

"And Dad asked me to take care of her if anything happened to her."

"So what happened?"

"I got cancer. The bad kind," Gloria answered, her voice a bit gravelly. "So Quinn came to take care of me. Doctors said I only had a year, but I'm still here."

Ronan put a hand on Ivy's shoulder. Her first instinct was to shrug it off, but she didn't. She liked that he'd offered it in support. As a way to lean on him.

Closing her eyes, she sighed, and then opened them. "I'm sorry for your trouble. I meant no offense."

Gloria gave her a little smile. "None taken. I know this is a bit of a shock for you."

"But it still doesn't answer the question of why all the demon activity."

Ronan squeezed her shoulder, then answered, "It's because of the key."

Quinn looked authentically surprised. "What key?"

"You know what I'm talking about." Ronan met her brother's gaze head-on as Quinn pushed off the table. She could feel the testosterone filling the room like a bad smell.

"Look, why don't the three of us go somewhere private and talk about this?" she suggested.

The frantic pounding of feet on the stairs interrupted them. A young scruffy-looking girl burst into the room. "Quinn, we need you down at checkpoint two."

Quinn sighed, then rubbed his face with both hands. "Okay, I'm coming." He looked at Ivy. "Why don't you get cleaned up?" He glanced at Ronan's bloody, wounded shoulder. "Take care of your guy here. And we'll talk when I get back." He headed for the stairs. "Bill, make sure they get some food, water and whatever else they need."

"Quinn, this is important," Ivy stated.

"So is keeping these people safe." He put a foot up on the first step. "Our conversation will keep for a couple of hours, I'm sure."

She watched him ascend the stairs, followed by almost everyone in the basement. Except for Gloria and the gunman named Bill.

Bill nodded to them. "Come with me and I'll find you some quarters and some food."

Ivy followed Bill up the stairs, Ronan right behind her.

Chapter 21

Ronan watched Ivy as she paced the room they'd been placed in. He wasn't ready to say imprisoned in, although there was someone stationed at their door available for anything they needed. Yeah, right, he thought. Available to keep them trapped inside was more like it.

"I hate waiting. It's been two hours. Where the hell is he?"

Ronan finished the bowl of stew they'd been given and dropped the plastic spoon into the garbage can. "He'll be here. He's probably trying to figure out the best way to lie to us about the key."

She stopped walking and frowned at him. "Do you think he'll deny he has it?"

He nodded. "Oh, yeah. It's why this town is under siege, I'm sure of it. So he'll try to keep it under wraps for as long as he can. Even though he knows I'm right."

She looked at him for a long moment. He could see she was struggling. It looked like she wanted to say something to him but was unsure how to put it. He had a notion of the thing she wanted to ask. Because he was asking himself the same question. Did it all start with him? Was he the reason that the demons had found out about Quinn and the key?

He decided to put her out of her misery. "The answer is, I don't know."

"What are you talking about?"

"The reason you're staring at me that way. You want to know if I think this is because of the cabal asking me to find the key."

"It's a reasonable question."

He nodded. "I know it is." He scratched at his chin where stubble was coming in. "But I do know that the cabal wouldn't want demons to have the key. So they didn't send them here. The demons are here on someone else's orders. Someone who knew that Quinn has the key and that he was here in Sumner." He rolled his shoulder, which was still stiff from the bullet wound, but healing nicely. "We didn't know that until fifteen hours ago. The demons have been here three days. They were here right around the time we first met."

"It can't be a coincidence."

"I agree. There are no such things as coincidences."

"What then?" She sighed, and he could see the fatigue lining her face.

"There's another player around. Someone with a lot of power and knowledge."

Ivy walked to the tiny cot in the corner and sank down onto it. She covered her face with her hands. "I hate this. I should be celebrating because I found my brother but all I have is a bad churning in my gut."

"Maybe it was the stew. It kind of has a bad aftertaste."

She lifted her head and half smiled at him. That's what he wanted to see. He didn't like seeing a defeated Ivy Strom. It almost scared him to see her like that. Like watching a steel bar bending under pressure.

"I'm sorry for the way Quinn treated you."

He waved her apology away. "Don't be. I expected it. I'm sure you did, as well."

She nodded. "Yeah, I guess I'd forgotten what a hard-ass he was."

"Just like another sibling I know."

Ronan got up from the chair, crossed the room

and sat down beside her on the cot. He put his arm around her shoulder and pulled her against him. She didn't resist, but laid her head on his shoulder. He liked that she could lean on him. He wanted her to. He wanted to be the man she could count on in good times or bad. He wanted...her.

"Yeah, families can be a hassle."

"Do you have a family? Brothers or sisters?" she asked. "I know virtually nothing about you." She closed her eyes, her head still on his shoulder.

He shook his head. "I lost them a long time ago."

"I'm sorry. How did it happen?"

He felt his throat tighten up. It was still so difficult to talk about it even after all these years. "It was the same night I became what I am."

"Are they dead?"

"Yeah," he sighed. He tried not to think about his mom and sister. They'd all been out for dinner together, in the wrong place at the wrong time, when he'd been attacked by the demons. They'd gotten in the way. He should've known his lifestyle would be the death of them eventually. He'd been drunk and stupid and they had paid the ultimate price for his mistakes.

"My mom and younger sister. They were with me at that restaurant and were walking with me through that alley to my car."

She wrapped her hands around his arm and held on to him as he continued. Her warmth pressed against him gave him the strength to talk about it without the guilt and anger and regret pulsing through him.

"For about five years after, I drank myself into oblivion almost every night. I thought maybe I could pollute the demon blood out of my system. And numb the pain of their deaths. But neither worked all that well."

"I tried that after my dad died," she murmured.

He sighed. "Yeah, it doesn't help, does it?"

"No, it doesn't." She lifted her head and stared him in the eyes. "I'm so sorry, Ronan, about what happened to you."

He nodded, and then brought his hand up to rub his thumb down her cheek. He tilted her face a little and leaned toward her mouth. She lifted her lips to his and they kissed.

Ivy brought her hands up to his chest and gripped his shirt, pulling him closer. She tore at his mouth, nipping and tugging on his tongue and lips with a savage glee. He responded in kind until they were both panting.

His heart pounded hard, as did his groin. He wanted to take her right here and now, their circumstances be damned. He didn't much care for anything, except Ivy. Kissing her, touching her, hearing her moan and feeling her writhe under his weight. But it was more than just the physical pulsing between them. He knew there was more than that. He knew she had feelings for him. As he harbored feelings for her. The question was, were they enough to get them through this together?

Unfortunately they didn't get a chance to find out before the door opened and Quinn marched in.

"Holy crap," he growled.

Ivy pulled away from Ronan and actually sprang to her feet.

"You have got to be kidding me." He shook his head. "Ivy, seriously?"

"Oh, please, spare me your ethics lesson," she growled back.

"Yeah, but him?" He gestured to Ronan. "He's practically a hellspawn."

That had Ronan on his feet. "You know if you want to solve this between us, I'm more than happy to take it to a more private venue."

Quinn took a step forward, his hands fisted.

Ivy got between them and pushed at Quinn. "Don't be an idiot." Then she poked Ronan in the chest. "And you relax. You aren't helping any."

"You know, I thought you'd gain some sense in the past three years. But I see you haven't. You're the same impulsive, unpredictable girl you were when I left."

Ivy pushed him again, and this time he backed up. "I have changed. More than you'll ever know. You made sure of that. You forced me to change by leaving. You abandoned me, Quinn. You left me to fend for myself. And I did." She bit out the last few words between clenched jaws. Waves of fury vibrated off her body.

Quinn's face fell. "Ivy, I didn't abandon you."

"The hell you didn't," she spat back. "What do you call sneaking out in the middle of the night with no notice, nothing but a note on the kitchen table telling me not to look for you? If that's not abandonment, then I don't know what is."

He ran a shaky hand through his hair. "That's not how I meant it. I just wanted to spare you some of Dad's shit that I had to deal with."

"Well, you didn't. Who do you think took up all the responsibility of hunting? Me." She poked him in the chest. "And I became a damn great hunter. No thanks to you."

"I'm sorry, Ivy. I didn't think my leaving would hurt you as much as it did."

She wanted to scream at him that it had ripped her heart out. What little of one she had left after Dad had died only a year before that. Instead she said, "Well, you're an idiot, aren't you?"

"It was just I always thought of you as pretty independent. You never needed my help in the past. I didn't think my presence meant all that much to you."

Tears stung the corners of her eyes, but she refused to let them fall. Not in front of Quinn and never in front of Ronan. So she dug her nails into the palms of her hands. "You thought wrong. I needed you, Quinn, especially after Dad died."

He reached out to her, setting his hand on her shoulder. "I'm sorry. I didn't know." She let him pull her into a hug. He patted her shoulders awkwardly.

After a few moments, she pulled back from him. "Okay, I sort of forgive you."

He smiled, and then punched her on the arm. "Good, because I don't how long I can be the mushy brother. It's totally cramping my style."

She returned his smile, not because she forgave him completely, but because she realized that she didn't need him in her life. She hadn't had to rely on him in years. She'd done it all on her own. She'd forged a life as an independent woman and made a name for herself in the hunting community. That wasn't to say she didn't want him around. She did. She loved her brother. She missed him. But she didn't need him to be who she was.

When she left this town, if he didn't come with her, she was okay with that because she knew he was alive and driven to complete his own mission.

She would be able to endure being separated from him…at least for a while.

"Okay, now we want to know about the key."

Quinn looked from her to Ronan and then back. "What do you know about it?"

"I've been told you have it," Ronan said. "And Quianna Lang informed us of its purpose."

He sighed, then asked, "How is Quianna?"

Ivy interrupted, "Who cares how she is? I want to know about this key."

"Ivy, you don't want to know. To know is to bring this," he gestured with his hands, "on you. It's important that I keep it hidden. If it fell into the wrong hands, it would be, well, nothing you can even imagine."

"I can imagine quite a bit."

"This war here in Sumner would be just the beginning. If the wrong person had the key and opened the chest—" he closed his eyes and shook his head "—it would literally be hell on earth. Those demons cannot be released."

"Who do you think is looking for it?" she asked.

Quinn stared straight at Ronan. "Besides the demons here in this town, I'd say you know perfectly well who wants it."

Ivy glanced at Ronan, then back to Quinn.

"You'd be right," Ronan said, his voice calm and flat.

"Who hired you?"

"Crimson Hall."

"The Crimson Hall Cabal?" He shook his head. "Jesus, they're worse than most of the demons in this town. Do you have any idea what they would do if they had the key?"

"I don't really care."

Ivy stepped between them. "He's not going to take it, Quinn. At first that was his plan, but that's changed." She glanced at Ronan for his confirmation.

Except Ronan made no motion to contradict Quinn. He just kept staring at her brother. He refused to make eye contact with her.

She stepped into his line of sight. "Right? You've changed your mind, right? It's not about that now."

He glanced down at her briefly, then dropped his gaze. "You don't understand, Ivy."

"You son of a bitch." Tears pricked the corners of her eyes. "I trusted you. I can't believe you're doing this for a few lousy thousands."

"It's not about money."

"What's it about then, huh?" She pushed him back. "Screwing me over?" She tried to shove him again, but his hands came up and locked around her wrists.

"This was never about you."

Those words stabbed her hard in the chest. The tears she was so desperately trying to hold back fell. She couldn't seize them any longer.

"I suggest you let go of my sister." Quinn's voice quivered with anger. Ronan let her go and took a distancing step away. Ivy turned to see Quinn leveling his gun at Ronan's head. "Now, we're going for a little walk."

"Don't kill him, Quinn." She hated the desperation in her voice.

Quinn frowned. "I'm not going to kill him. But he's no longer welcome in this compound."

"Where are you going to take him?"

"Back to town. He can fend for himself."

Quinn motioned with his gun to the door. Ronan walked to it, seemingly unaffected. Ivy always thought he was stoic and unflinching, but she'd never seen him so cold. It was as if *he* was made of ice.

"Shooting me won't do you any good," Ronan said as he neared the door. "I can heal myself pretty fast. Benefit of my demon blood."

"Yeah, I bet." Quinn snorted. "Except I'm pretty sure you'd have a harder time healing if I put this silver bullet in your head."

Ronan nodded. "Yeah, that might hurt a little more."

"Open the door and go out," Quinn ordered.

Ronan did as he instructed and moved out of the room. Quinn followed, Ivy behind him, still unsure of what she was doing or how she was feeling.

She followed them all the way out onto the driveway of the farmhouse. There Quinn had two of his gunmen standing by to take Ronan away.

They were about to hood him when Ivy stepped forward. "Wait."

She went to stand in front of Ronan. "Tell me this wasn't *all* for money." She needed to know that he'd felt something for her. That the passion between them hadn't been fake. That he hadn't just slept with her to get to her brother and the key.

"It was never for money. The cabal has a cure. I need the key to exchange for it." He lifted his hand and traced a finger down her cheek. "I needed you at first, but then, I—"

"Doesn't matter why," Quinn interrupted. "You're still a traitor."

Ronan dropped his hand and straightened. "I'm sorry, Ivy. I never meant to hurt you."

She glared at him for a long while, her heart snapping in two. "Don't worry about it. You didn't." She lifted her chin, then walked back to stand beside her brother. Although her legs quivered like jelly, she stood straight and tall.

One of the gunmen shackled Ronan's wrists behind his back and pulled a hood over his head.

Then they grabbed him and tossed him in the backseat of a Chevy POS.

Ivy stood in the driveway and watched them drive away. Quinn holstered his gun and turned to her. He touched her on the shoulder, much like Ronan had done before when he knew she was feeling sad. "Are you okay with this?"

She shrugged off his hand. "Yeah, why wouldn't I be?"

"I just thought, you had, you know, strong feelings for him or something."

"He was a job and nothing more. He helped me get here, which was what I wanted. End of story." She turned and started for the house. "Now, tell me how I get to kill some demons."

Chapter 22

They dumped Ronan out into a ditch just outside the other end of town. Although they'd taken several turns and backtracked a few times, he still had an idea how to get back to the compound. He'd just had to cross the demon-infested town to do it.

Still shackled, he rolled onto his knees then pressed to his feet. He leaned over and shook the bag off his head. He'd been right; he was on the outskirts of the town. He could see the scattering of houses as they pressed together to start the town limits.

Now to take care of these handcuffs.

Closing his eyes and concentrating as hard as he could, Ronan conjured a ball of heat in his body.

He moved it up to his shoulders, down his arms and into his wrists. Gritting his teeth, he poured all he had into his hands. Within another two minutes, the metal started to melt. He could feel it drip off his wrists until, finally, he yanked his hands free of their bindings.

Wincing, he looked down at his wrists. They were raw and red, blisters starting to form. Thankfully it wouldn't last long. After an hour or two his skin should be healed.

He checked his surroundings. There was no one around. It looked like about a two-mile hike back into town. He had no weapons but he figured he'd find some on the way. After cracking his sore neck, he started to jog on the dirt road.

It didn't take him long to reach town. He hunkered down inside a burned-out building along Main Street and took stock of the situation. He found a knife on the floor in the building; he pocketed it. He also found an aluminum bat that might come in handy.

Peering through the broken and black window, he spotted about six people out on the street. Two appeared to be demons, not the same ones as before, and the other four were of the possessed persuasion. He hated dealing with the possessed. Because he didn't have any exorcist tools with him, no salt, no silver, no bible, he couldn't relieve the human hosts of their parasites. So if they came after him, he had to take them down without prejudice.

Ronan watched as the two demons conversed on the street. One was talking into a radio and then relaying information to the other. It looked like a serious conversation. The one on the radio pointed to various points along the street. It appeared they were planning something. He needed to get closer so he could hear exactly what.

Slowly, silently, he crept out of the building through the busted door. He crouched against the wall for a minute, then continued on. He spotted an abandoned car about six feet behind the demon duo. If he could get to it, he'd be able to hear them, but he had to cross an open part of the street to get there.

Looking up at the buildings, he searched for snipers or scouts on the roofs. He didn't see any. He glanced down the street, looking for any sign of more demons or the possessed. As far as he could tell, the road was eerily quiet and void of more problems.

Still, it felt like the calm before the storm.

Under his breath, he counted to three, then shot across the street, mindful of where he stepped. He made it to the car and crouched down behind it. He sighed with relief, then crept along the metal body and planted himself near the bumper, just out of the line of sight of the two demons. But he was close enough now to hear every word.

"They kicked the cambion out," the radio demon said.

The other one nodded. "No surprise considering the Stroms' reputation. I was surprised to hear that the bitch Ivy Strom had been partnered with him to begin with."

"Well, true to form, she cut him loose. I was surprised that she didn't kill him." Radio demon smiled. "I almost admire her cold, calculated ways. It's almost going to be a shame to kill her."

The other demon smiled. "We could play with her first."

"True."

And they laughed together.

It took all Ronan had not to come up behind them both and jam his knife into their throats. He had to be patient. He would get his chance soon enough, he was sure.

The radio crackled in the demon's hand. He pushed a button and spoke. "Yes?"

Ronan couldn't hear what was said through the radio.

But after a few seconds the radio demon said to the other with a satisfied grin, "We have their location. In an hour we will be happily feasting on the Stroms' blood. They don't stand a chance."

"Does he think they have any idea they have a traitor in the camp?"

Radio demon shook his head. "He says they are dumber than a sack of hammers. He says instead of kicking out the cambion, they should've been looking at those closest to Quinn Strom."

They both laughed again.

"When are we moving out?"

"Right away. The rendezvous point is three blocks from here at the old church."

Ronan had heard enough. He knew what he had to do. Slipping his knife out of his belt, he pushed away from the car and rushed the demons.

He had the radio demon's chin in his hand and his neck exposed in two seconds flat. The knife went in nice and easy. After dispatching him, he let go and reached for the other. But the demon was already on the move.

Gripping his knife tight in his right hand, Ronan took off at a run in pursuit.

After a briefing with her brother about their current demon situation, Ivy stepped outside for a breather. She wandered down to the barn and around the other side. There she found a tree stump that was perfect for sitting. She took a swig from the bottle of water she'd taken with her, then set it down on the ground.

No matter how much liquid she drank, she still felt hollow and thirsty. She knew it had nothing to do with being dehydrated. No, it had everything to do with a certain cambion.

She understood her brother had to make a decision for the compound. And she knew he honestly believed it was the right one, but Ivy couldn't help thinking it had been a stupid one. Quinn thought he was protecting his people, but she felt they would've been better off with Ronan here in the camp.

And she supposed she wanted him here for other reasons, as well.

Although his admission about still wanting the key stung her, she still couldn't stop the feelings she had for him. She couldn't stop her heart from beating fast when she thought about him. Or halt the way her belly flipped and her thighs clenched when she remembered his lips on her skin, his hands sliding up and down her body.

No amount of water was going to fill up the hole that had been ripped inside her.

She took another drink anyway.

Standing, she decided to go back into the house. Maybe she'd track Quinn down and ask him to reconsider his decision about Ronan. Maybe she'd ask to be dumped in the same place they'd dumped him.

Her brother didn't need her. He was doing just fine on his own. Here she thought she was coming to rescue him, that he was in need of her help, but the reality was he'd never really needed her.

And as it was, she'd finally realized she didn't need him. She was okay on her own. She was actually more than okay. But she wasn't really alone, was she? She could have Ronan at her side if she wanted.

Truth be told, she did want that, despite his decision to take the key. He needed it. To get a cure to his cambionism. She understood that desire to fix who he was. How many times had she wished she could fix the defects in herself? But what she wanted to say to Ronan was that he was fine the way he was. The demon blood inside him didn't alter who he truly was. She wished she could show him how incredible he was, as is.

She made her way around the barn and was about to head up to the farmhouse when something flashed at her out of the corner of her eye. Without looking directly, she turned her head a little, as if studying the tree next to her.

There it was again. A flash of metal. A gun, she suspected. Someone was hunkered down in the tall grass in the field beyond the compound. They were under attack.

Ivy ran the rest of the way to the house, bursting through the door and locking it behind her. She found Quinn in the kitchen at the table going over a map of the town.

"They're here. We're under attack."

"Are you sure?" he asked, already folding up the map.

"Deadly sure."

He nodded to the others in the kitchen. "All right, arm yourselves. Everyone to their points. Just like we planned." He looked at Gloria. "Get the children in the cellar."

Gloria ran out of the room already calling for the kids that were in and around the camp.

Quinn tossed Ivy a shotgun. "You're with me."

"We should split up. I'm a good shot. You can use me to our advantage."

He looked at her for a moment and she thought maybe he was going to argue with her, but he finally nodded. "You're right. You aren't a little girl anymore."

"I haven't been for a long while."

"Okay, take the west point. Bill, go with Ivy. Take three others with you."

Before they separated, Ivy grabbed Quinn's

arm. "Even though I'm still angry at you, I love you, you damn idiot."

He smiled and kissed her quick on top of the head, like he used to when she was little. "Love you, too, pain in my ass."

Pumping a round into the chamber, Ivy looked at Bill and the others. "Let's go kill some demons."

Chapter 23

It didn't take the demons long before they stormed the farmhouse. But like the cowards they were, they sent in their possessed counterparts. Regular people who had no clue what they were doing. Puppets for the demons to play with.

For the townspeople with Ivy, it was difficult for them to watch as their loved ones and neighbors sprang at them from the tall grass firing rifles or wielding pipes and bats that they would no doubt use to bash their heads in. So for that reason, Quinn had given every group tranquilizer guns as well as regular weapons.

At a distance it proved difficult to tell who was a demon and who was just possessed, so Ivy just started shooting everyone she could see with tranquilizer darts. One by one the attackers fell. They would be out for at least twelve hours, which would give Quinn time to go out and do a mass exorcism.

The first wave came and went, with about ten people charging toward the west corner where Ivy, Bill and a couple of others were stationed behind two beat-up pickup trucks. But she knew that was just the beginning. She knew an all-out offensive when she saw one, and this was it. The demons were sending out everything they had.

Ivy reloaded her shotgun and the tranquilizer, her heart sinking. She glanced at Bill. "We only have five darts left."

He sighed. "What do you think we should do?"

"I don't know. We can't really start shooting townspeople. We could kill someone."

"We need someone up front to take them out with a bat or something as they advance."

She nodded. Made sense. Unless of course the possessed had a gun; a bat wasn't going to stop the bullet.

"I'll go," Bill said.

"Are you sure?"

He nodded. "I know these people. If I don't recognize someone I'll be more discerning." He lifted his gun.

"Okay, good luck."

With a nod to her and the other two, Bill slid around the side of one of the trucks, and then ran across the yard to a spot near the house behind some hay bales.

He got in position just in time for another wave of people to jump out of the tall grass and run screaming and grunting across the gravel driveway, brandishing all manner of weapons. Ivy picked up the tranquilizer and waited to see how Bill fared. If she needed to, she would put down anyone that got past him and hope for the best.

She held her breath as two men holding tire irons rushed toward Bill like madmen. She wouldn't have been surprised to see foam spilling out between their lips. The looks in their eyes were ones of pure madness. As they approached, getting closer and closer, she picked up the dart gun and set her sights.

Then it all went wrong.

She lowered the dart gun and cursed up a storm. "Son of a bitch!"

"What?" The guy called Stewart or Chuck, she couldn't really remember which, grabbed her arm. His eyes were as wide as dollar coins.

But she didn't have time to answer him. She swatted his hand away, and then pushed him to the back of the truck. "Move." He did, so did the other guy. They had no choice really, because she was forcing them forward.

"What's going on?" the guy asked. "Did something happen to Bill?"

"Yeah, he switched sides."

Both their mouths gaped.

Ivy ignored them and surveyed the situation. They had to move from their position or risk getting pinned down. She saw an outbuilding about ten yards to their right, but they had to cross the open yard to get there. It was a risk they had to take because staying where they were was going to get them killed.

She grabbed Stewart/Chuck by the shirt lapels. "Look, we need to cross the yard to that building. Can you do that?"

He nodded, but she still wasn't sure he was listening. He had that glazed-over shiny look in his eyes. But she couldn't wait to see if he truly got it or not. They had to move now.

"On my count."

They both looked at her expectantly.

"One, two…"

Stewart/Chuck didn't wait until three. He dashed across the yard. Sounds of gunfire exploded around them. And Stewart/Chuck went down. The other guy had been right behind him. Now he turned to dive back, but it was too late.

He got nicked by a bullet in the leg and collapsed, grabbing at his knee and screaming wildly.

Ivy swore again, and was about to rush out and see if she could pull the injured man behind the truck, but the press of metal into the back of her head made her stop.

"Drop your weapons." It was Bill behind her, stabbing the gun into her skull.

She tossed the shotgun down.

"And the tranq gun."

She pulled that out of her waistband and tossed it to the ground. "You're a traitor to your species, Bill. How does that feel?"

"You tell me. You're the one sleeping with a cambion." He grabbed her by the shoulder and pulled her to her feet.

It took everything she had not to turn around and jam her blade into his big gut. But she stayed still. She could feel the barrel of his gun quiver a little. Obviously, Bill wasn't too sure about his convictions.

"He's dead, by the way," he said, as if she'd asked about the weather. "Had his neck slit down on Main Street. He thought he could take some of them out. But he was no match for them."

She started to shake then. She bit down on her lip, trying hard not to scream, or rage, or turn around and scream in his face that he was a big fat liar. There was no way anyone had gotten the better of Ronan. She knew it in her heart. She wasn't going to let anyone, especially not this traitorous piece of crap, tell her otherwise.

"What did the demons promise you to do this? To kill your own people?" she asked.

"Everything I want."

She shook her head, still mindful of the gun pressed against it. "So you sold your soul for what, some money, a fast car, a hot vacation spot and some ass? Seems pretty lame to me."

"Shut up!" He kicked her in the back of the knee, sending her to the ground. She landed on her hands. "Keep talking and I'll put a bullet in your empty head."

Ivy pushed up to her knees but kept her hands down on her thighs. She had a knife tucked into her boot. If she could get to it, she'd embed it into Bill's femur. "Okay, Bill. No need to get angry. I'll shut up."

He grabbed her again, this time by the hair. He pulled her back up to her feet, keeping the gun pressed to her skull. He turned her around and marched her out into the main yard in front of the house where she knew Quinn had stationed himself.

There was a lot of commotion going on as he led her to the front. The others hadn't seen Bill's betrayal yet; they were still busy holding off their own sieges, manning their stations. Screams could be heard around them, and Ivy felt a bullet whiz by her left arm as they marched around the corner.

"Quinn!" Bill yelled. "Quinn, I have your sister!"

And just like that, all the commotion stopped. Bill had gotten everyone's attention with that little piece of information.

He pushed her forward to face the house. "Quinn, I know you're there. I know you can see her. If I don't see you in five seconds I'm going to blow her pretty head apart."

It was exactly four seconds before Quinn's head popped up from behind the trellis on the roof of the house. Ivy was loath to admit that she breathed a little sigh of relief when she saw him.

"What do you want?" Quinn asked.

"Complete surrender."

Quinn looked at her. Even from the distance she could see the pure agony on his face. The agony of the decision he had to make. "Ivy?"

She knew what he was asking. If she could take Bill out without getting killed in the process. She gauged the situation. The only weapon she had now was the blade in her boot. She'd used the others along the way. There was no way she could get to her weapon before Bill pulled the trigger. And even if she could somehow elbow him in the gut or take out his kneecap with a good kick, he'd likely mortally wound her even if it wasn't a head shot.

If Ronan had been here, with his healing hands, she might've considered it. But as it was, she didn't see a way out of this right now.

"No," she finally said.

"No, what?" He knocked her in the head with his gun. "No, what, bitch?"

Quinn stood all the way. "You have my surrender."

"I'll believe you when I see you face-to-face without any weapons."

"Fine. We're coming down. No one do anything stupid."

She knew he not only said that for Bill's benefit but for the rest of the compound. She'd counted about ten weapons trained on her and Bill the second they'd stepped into the front yard.

About three minutes later, the front door opened and Quinn walked out, his hands out to the side, showing that they were empty. He came down the front-stoop steps.

"I'm unarmed."

Bill snorted. "I highly doubt that, Strom, but as long as I have baby sister here, I know you won't do anything dumb." Then he put his fingers in his mouth and let out a high-pitched whistle.

Eight demons stepped out of the tall grass and shadows surrounding the compound and walked into view. They were all smiles. One of them, a redheaded woman, stepped up next to Ivy. She ran her hand down Ivy's arm.

"Two Stroms for the price of one." She laughed. "It's a great day."

Chapter 24

Ronan stayed hidden behind the silo in the field about one hundred yards from the farmhouse. He wouldn't do Ivy any good by prematurely jumping out and revealing his position. He had the element of surprise on his side and he was going to use it to his advantage.

Earlier, he'd lost the second demon through the town streets, but it had brought him closer to the demon rendezvous. Because of his superior hearing and vision he'd been able to overhear exactly what was going on from his spot. He knew they were planning an attack on the human compound. He also knew they had an inside man. Someone close to Quinn who'd been feeding them vital information this whole time.

And because of their misplaced confidence in their strength and cunningness, Ronan had been able to follow them to the farmhouse.

They'd known he'd been kicked out of the camp but they'd misjudged his willingness to return and help the humans. To save Ivy. He supposed the demons had no concept of loyalty, friendship or love.

Yeah, he had to admit it to himself. He was in love with her. It probably wouldn't change her mind about him, though. And he didn't blame her. Despite everything, despite how he felt about her, he still needed the key. He wished she could understand that. His need to be fully human again. And if this was the only way, he'd do it.

Through the binoculars he'd procured from one of Ivy's bags that he'd gone back to their busted-up car to retrieve, he watched as the demons herded Ivy, Quinn and all the others into the farmhouse. He imagined they would secure them in the basement. Now he just needed to get close enough to use the other goodies Ivy had in her gear.

Some of the things that she'd invented for demon hunting were inspired to be sure.

Once they were all inside, leaving two sentries out front, the possessed he assumed, Ronan hefted the pack over his shoulder and crawled his way across the field. He was wearing black so he knew he was somewhat camouflaged in the waning light. He just had to keep his patience and go slowly and carefully. Although everything inside him screamed at him to run and attack and kill everyone standing in the way between him and Ivy, he took in a few deep breaths and tried to stay calm and levelheaded.

There was a thick copse of trees on the east side of the house. He would get there, and then plan the best way to get in without killing any of the possessed. And save Ivy. He knew it was going to be damn near impossible on all fronts, but he had to try.

It was a long, arduous crawl, but Ronan finally made it to the edge of the trees. Cast in shadow among the tall oaks, he could get around easier. He crept along the tree line and crouched behind a large oak directly opposite one of the guards.

He knew there were two guards at the front of the house; he suspected there would be at least two more in the back. Unzipping the duffel bag, Ronan took out a modified rifle. He screwed on a front piece that looked like a silencer. It was, in fact, a housing for plastic bullets. He didn't know where Ivy got them, probably an army surplus store somewhere, but it was ingenious for taking out those you didn't want to kill—just incapacitate.

Once he took out the side guard, he had to be on the run toward the house to take out the others. He wanted to go in as silently as possible. If the demons knew he was coming, they might panic and kill everyone inside. He had some time, he knew. Quinn wouldn't give the key up easily. Ronan suspected they'd have to torture him for a while first.

He lined up the sights on the rifle. He had to hit the guard in the head to knock him unconscious. Anywhere else would just be damaging but not enough to incapacitate. The guard could still cry out to the others.

Ronan was cautious about using the plastic bullets. He knew there had been deaths in the past from precisely this—hits to the head. But there was no other way of taking the guy out from a distance. He'd get in closer for the others. But this first one had to be done this way. Muttering a prayer under his breath, he put his finger on the trigger and pulled.

The bullet hit the guard right in the temple, exactly where Ronan had aimed. He went down like a ton of bricks, sinking to the ground without a word. One down.

Ronan picked up the bag and ran to the corner of the house. He grabbed the fallen guard's feet and dragged him to the porch, rolling him under it. He then hopped over the railing and onto the porch. He crept along the wall to the other corner and peered over. The guard was there, a woman this time, holding a shotgun. He reached into the bag and grabbed something for close encounters. A stun gun.

He set down the bag, then walked to the end of the porch and leaned over the railing. "Hey." He ducked back around so she couldn't shoot him outright. Crouching, he watched through the porch rails for her to appear. He only had to wait ten seconds.

Her eyes widened when she spotted him and she raised her weapon, but Ronan was faster. He had the stun gun through the rails and pressed the button. The two wires sprang out and attached to her cheek. Electricity zipped through the lines and into the woman's body. She was down on the ground in seconds.

Grabbing the bag, he jumped over the railing, landing softly by the downed guard's body. He rolled her under the porch, then picked up her shotgun and shoved it into the duffel bag. As quick as he could, he ran along the side of the house to the back. He did a quick peek around the corner. He'd assumed right. There were two guards manning the back.

Before he could consider how he was going to dispatch them, the guard closest to him came around the corner, unzipping his jeans to relieve himself. Ronan snuck up behind him, put his arm around his neck and choked him out. He dragged him to the side and laid him up against the wall. One more to go before he could get into the house and get Ivy out.

Pressed against the side wall, Ronan waited until the perfect opportunity to take out the other guard. It came about five minutes later when he wandered over to find out what happened to his buddy.

"Joe," the guard called, "where you at?"

Ronan waited until he was right in front of him, then he sprang into action. But he made a vital error. The guard wasn't one of the possessed, but a demon.

He swatted away Ronan's arm and smiled. "Hello, sunshine."

Chapter 25

Ivy wriggled her hands back and forth trying to loosen the ropes around her wrists. She was bound to a chair in the middle of the basement—the same spot she'd been in earlier when she and Ronan had been picked up. Quinn was bound to another chair beside her. The rest of their people had been herded into a corner by the demons. Unfortunately there were only six of them left.

The demon horde, what was left of them at least, were piled in the room as well, all lined up to take a shot at Quinn. They wanted to know where the key was. So far, her brother was keeping mum. But she suspected that would get harder to do as the demons got more creative with their questions. Luckily, the questions had been just that, questions. No painful torture to accompany them. Not yet, anyway. She suspected that was soon in coming.

Very soon, by the malevolent gleam in the current interrogator's black eyes.

He leaned into Quinn's face, likely breathing his foul sulfuric breath onto him. "You do realize we're going to torture you to find out the location of the key, don't you?"

"Whatever, hellspawn," Quinn spat. "Give me your best shot."

Smiling, the demon clenched his fist and wound back, then hit Quinn across the nose. Ivy could hear the definitive sickening crack of cartilage as Quinn's head snapped back.

She had to bite her tongue to stop from cursing the demon. Her insults and anger weren't going to help Quinn. It might, in fact, make it worse for him. When he swung his head back around, blood gushed from his nose and soaked his shirt. She closed her eyes and swore under her breath. She pulled at her hands a little more. If only she could get free.

All the demons laughed at Quinn's busted nose and swollen lip. One female stepped forward and ran a finger over his lips, gathering his blood onto it.

She sucked the crimson liquid off and sighed happily. "Demon-hunter blood is the sweetest thing."

Quinn cursed at her. But it didn't stop her from taking more from him.

Ivy couldn't hold back her fury any longer. She kicked out with her right leg at the demoness. She struck the demoness in the back of the thigh. It sent the demoness stumbling sideways.

This made the other demons laugh again.

The demoness swung around and glared at Ivy. It made her sick to see Quinn's blood staining her lips and teeth. Ivy had to swallow down the bile rising in her throat.

The demoness moved toward her, coming around the back of the chair. She gripped the back of Ivy's head, yanking on her hair, pulling her head back. "You know, I think we've been doing this the wrong way. We could beat on Quinn all day and he wouldn't tell us, but if we beat on baby sister…"

Quinn erupted, pulling on his restraints. "You leave her alone! I'll rip you apart if you touch her!"

And that was the absolutely worst thing he could've ever said. Now they knew without a shadow of a doubt that torturing Ivy would work wonders on Quinn's tongue.

She looked at Quinn, wanting to smack him across the head. He knew better. "Don't be stupid."

The demoness leaned down into her face. "I think it's well past that point, don't you, darling?"

Ivy spat at her.

The demoness wiped the gob away, then twisted her hand in Ivy's hair and yanked even harder. Pain shot over her skull. She wondered how painful it would be if the demoness ripped all her hair out. Probably agony. She shivered just thinking about it.

Another demon, the male that had struck Quinn, sauntered over to where Ivy was held. He stood in front of her, openly leering down at her. Her stomach roiled at the lecherous look in his black eyes.

"How about we play with her first?" He kicked at her legs, driving them apart. "I've never screwed a demon hunter before."

The demoness shook her head. "That's all you think about, isn't it?"

He shrugged. "I can't help it. I am a lust demon, after all."

Ivy struggled in her chair, flailing her legs at him. "I'll rip it off before you even get it near me."

He laughed, and then grabbed both her legs. "You're fun." He pushed her backwards.

Her chair toppled over with her in it. She hit the

hard floor, the back of her head smacking painfully against the cement. Her scalp throbbed like an acid burn, and when she saw strands of her black hair in the demoness's hand, she understood why.

"You stupid fool," the demoness berated the other.

Ivy let them argue because her fall had done two wonderful things. It had broken one of the spokes in the chair back and it had loosened her ropes. Without bringing attention to herself, she managed to pull one of her hands free.

She looked at Quinn and winked.

He started to struggle in his chair, bouncing up and down and kicking his legs. "I'll kill you! I'll kill you all!" He yelled so loud it made her ears hurt. "You'll never find the key!"

But it did the job. It got the attention of all the demons. All the focus was on Quinn, so no one noticed, at least for the first three seconds, when Ivy rolled to her knees and scrambled to her feet.

"Run, Ivy!" Quinn screamed as he launched himself, chair strapped to his body, at the closest demon to the stairwell, affording her a small window of escape.

She took it. As fast as she could, she sprinted toward the stairs. She was on the bottom step when the demoness came up behind her and grabbed at her hair again.

"I'm going to scalp you alive," the demoness growled.

"Hell, no, you won't."

There was a distinctive popping noise, and something round and silver split the demoness's face. Shrieking, she clawed at her bubbling forehead and scrambled backwards.

Ivy looked up the stairwell to see Ronan on the top, holding her modified paintball gun. It shot quicksilver-filled pellets instead of paint-filled ones.

She nearly fainted with relief to see him.

"Duck," he ordered.

She dropped to the stairs as he lobbed two homemade holy-water grenades into the basement. She heard them bounce once, then not only heard the percussion but also felt it as they exploded into a thousand plastic pieces. Holy water exploded everywhere. It even soaked the back of her jeans.

There was a lot of screaming and moaning in the basement when she turned to look at the damage. Demons fumbled around, shrieking and clawing at their melting and bubbling faces, hands, arms, any place that there had been exposed skin.

She pushed off the stairs and went back into the room. She picked up a gun that had fallen from one of the demon's mangled hands and pumped a round into him. He fell silent to the floor. She turned and shot another one in the face.

By this time, Ronan was down at her side, dispatching the rest. The other humans had jumped into the action, and there were demon parts flying all over the place.

Ivy ran to where Quinn still sat bound in the chair. She untied his hands from behind his back. "Are you okay?"

He nodded. "I think I got speared by shrapnel, though."

She glanced down and saw a growing blood spot on the denim on his thigh. He pulled open the rip in his jeans to show a small piece of plastic sticking into his flesh. As carefully as he could, he pulled it out and tossed it to the floor.

"It's just a flesh wound," Ivy pronounced, which made Quinn laugh. It was an old joke from their childhood and the many Monty Python film festivals they partook in over the years.

She helped him stand and he hugged her tight. "Are you okay?"

She nodded. "My head hurts, but I probably just have a bump or two."

They broke apart, then both turned to look at Ronan. He was busy helping the other captives up the stairs. He paused in what he was doing and looked at them. "There are a bunch of possessed

out there that need exorcising. The other two demons ran for it."

Quinn limped over to the table along the wall;
he picked up his bible, a holy water ampul and his
cross. He crossed the room, and then brushed past
Ronan as he climbed the stairs.

When he was gone, when they were all gone,
Ivy moved toward Ronan. He stood waiting for
her at the bottom of the steps.

"You saved me. Again."

He smiled. "Yeah, you owe me big-time."

"They said you were dead."

"Lies. As you can tell, I'm quite alive."

Tears brewing in her eyes, she moved forward
and wrapped her arms around him, burying her
face into his shoulder. She breathed in the now-
familiar scent of him and sighed.

He dropped the paintball gun and wrapped
his arms around her, as well. His hands pressed
against her back, holding her, possessing her. And
she felt right and secure and safe for one of the
first times in her whole life.

"I'm sorry," she breathed into his shoulder.

He brought his other hand up to her neck and
cradled her head. "Don't be. It wasn't you that
drove me out."

"I know, but I didn't stop him."

He sighed. "I didn't expect you to. He's your

brother. He's your kin. Blood will always be thicker than water. I know that all too well."

She pulled back then and looked at him. She brought a hand up to his face and touched his cheek. "You're wrong, Ronan. You have more humanity than anyone I've ever known. You are the good guy. You're the hero of this story."

"And what does that make you?"

She stretched up to his face and pressed her lips to his, whispering against them, "The sexy love interest."

He tilted her head ever so slightly with his hand at her neck and deepened the kiss. The kiss was slow, and hot, and wet and the most perfect thing Ivy had ever experienced.

Until a voice from above ruined the moment.

"If you two can break apart for a minute, I need your help reviving the townspeople."

Ivy looked up the staircase at Quinn, who was standing up top, a deep frown on his face and impatience in his voice.

"Give us a few minutes, okay, Quinn? We have some unfinished business to take care of."

Quinn made a disgusted noise, then said, "Jesus, Ivy, can't you save it for later?"

That made her laugh, and taking Ronan's hand in hers, she mounted the stairs with the cambion right beside her all the way.

Chapter 26

It took the three of them over four hours to exorcise everyone that needed it and to carry out and burn the dead demons. They dug a ditch, filled it with the bodies, salted it, did the last rites and then burned the lot. Fixing the town was going to take weeks, months even. Time Ronan didn't have or was willing to give.

When it was done, the three of them sat in the kitchen and drank whatever alcohol was available. Quinn had a beer, Ivy some scotch and Ronan had vodka on ice. After the fourth one he was starting to feel calm and controlled.

They hadn't talked much, but after an hour of

straight drinking, Quinn broke the awkward silence.

He held out his beer bottle toward Ronan. "I misjudged you. I'm sorry for that."

Ronan clinked his glass to the bottle. "I'll take it."

They both drank, then Quinn said, "If Ivy thinks you're good people, then I'm inclined to listen to her."

"For once," Ivy interjected.

Quinn smiled. "Yes, for once."

"Which means, I guess I have to listen to her when she says that you're not such a bad guy."

"Yup, I guess you will."

They all clinked their respective containers, and then downed whatever was left in them. Ivy grabbed the scotch bottle and poured more into her glass.

"I have to say, I'm happy they didn't get a chance to torture me to get info from you, Quinn."

He nodded. "Me, too."

"Do you think you would've told them where the key was?"

He shrugged. "Probably." He looked at her, and Ronan could see the love there for her. Quinn would've gone to hell and back for her.

Quinn started to chuckle. "It's ironic, really.

The whole time they're asking for the key and it was right there in front of their faces."

Ivy frowned. "What? What do you mean? Where is it?"

He reached across the table and hooked a finger into the chain around Ivy's neck. He tugged a little, and the heavy silver cross she always wore close to her skin popped out from her T-shirt. He let it go and smiled.

She looked down and wrapped her hand around the cross. "Are you serious?"

He nodded. "I had the key encased in silver and fashioned as a cross."

Ronan looked at the necklace, just as surprised as Ivy. It was very clever on Quinn's part.

"I had it the whole time?" Ivy asked incredulously.

"Yup. I thought, what better way to hide it than in the open? Who would've thought to look for it around your neck?"

She dropped her hand and leaned back in her chair. "And here I went and brought it right to them."

"You didn't know, Ivy. It's not your fault. How could you have known?"

"Was this the real reason you left?"

He nodded. "One of them. I thought it would be safe with you, especially if I wasn't around. And especially since I disguised it so well." He shook his head. "I just didn't expect you to come find me after three years." He touched her on the shoulder. "You're a persistent one, aren't you?"

"Yeah, too persistent, obviously."

"The good thing is the key is safe and so are you. That's all that matters now."

She smiled at him, then took a hefty swallow of scotch.

Quinn lifted his drink toward Ronan. "Thanks to you, that is. You saved the day, my friend."

Ronan filled his glass again and downed the whole thing. He set the empty glass on the table, his hand slightly trembling. Ivy reached across the table and covered it with hers. She looked at Ronan with that way of hers. There was a twinkle in her eye that made his gut clench.

"Now that that's been taken care of—" She stood and grabbed his hand. "Ronan and I need to have a little chat."

Quinn shook his head with a half smile. He nodded toward the back hallway. "There're clean sheets in the room down the hall."

Laughing, Ivy pulled Ronan down the hallway to the room. She kicked open the door and pulled him through. Before he was even fully in the room, she pounced on him, pushing him up against the back of the door. She kissed him hard, her hands everywhere at once.

Then she dropped to her knees, her fingers on the zipper of his pants. Slowly, she drew the zipper down, then tugged his pants down his legs. His erection strained against the cotton of his shorts. She rubbed him through the fabric, driving him mad with each stroke.

He banged his head back on the wall as she slowly, agonizingly drew him out. Her hand wrapped around him, she tickled the tip with her tongue.

"Damn, woman, are you trying to kill me?" he cursed under his breath as she licked him over and over, teasing him until he was as hard as steel.

"I see I've found your weakness," she said between licks.

He dug his fingers into the wall behind him. "Yeah, you."

She looked up at him beneath the hood of her lashes. It was a surprised look, a solemn one. He hadn't meant to say it out loud but she'd driven him to it. Everything about her drove him insane with desire. Lost to more emotions than he wanted to feel. But there it was and there was nothing he could do about it.

Gripping him tight, she slid him into her mouth. He watched as she stroked him, soft then hard alternately. He could feel the light scrape of her teeth on his sensitive flesh and the gentle teasing of her tongue. It was enough to drive him over the edge.

"Ivy," he panted.

"Don't talk," she said around him. "Just feel."

Ronan reached down, grabbed her under the arms and hefted her to her feet. Wrapping a hand in her tumble of hair, he spun her around and slammed her up against the wall. He kicked out of his pants and shorts and nudging her legs apart, settled in between them.

He put his other hand down between them and undid her pants. He tugged at them until, finally, she helped him out and shimmied out of them, kicking them across the room. He slid his fingers under the waistband of her pretty panties and yanked, rending them in half. He jerked a little harder and was able to get them all the way off. He tossed the torn lace over his shoulder.

Growling low in his throat, he moved in and crushed his mouth to hers. The kiss left him lightheaded, unstable. Ronan trailed his hands down her back and molded the firm cheeks of her ass, and then he picked her up. Ivy spread her legs and wrapped them around him. Gripping her tightly, he nibbled on her bottom lip, nipping and teasing, and made his way over her chin to her neck. The taste of her skin tingled in his mouth.

He nuzzled in between her legs, pinning her against the wall with his body. With the warm, wet heat of her center pressed against his erection, he thought he'd died and gone to heaven. Finally, he'd made it.

His muscles, from feet to head, trembled with desire, a ferocious, insatiable hunger. He needed to be inside Ivy now. The waiting was ripping him to pieces from the inside out.

He licked the side of her neck and nibbled on her ear. "I can't hold back for much longer."

"Then don't," she panted.

Her body quivered under his touch. He could feel the beating of her heart next to his, hard, fierce and frantic. All the things he felt for her and more.

One hand balanced her against the wall. The other he moved down between them and gripped his shaft tight, to guide him to her. Moving his hand up, he sought her. She was deliciously hot and wet and ready. Control fraying at the edges, he buried his entire length inside her with one swift thrust.

Gripping his shoulders hard, Ivy held on as he drove her up, reveling in how strong he was. Every nerve ending in her body sparked to life as he moved, slowly at first, then picked up his pace before finding a fiery tempo that sent shivers from her toes to her scalp.

She moved her head and found his mouth, diving her tongue between his lips. She kissed him with the fervor and passion that bubbled up inside her. She was ravenous for him.

He pounded between her legs as they kissed. With each thrust, Ivy thought she'd go insane with pleasure. It didn't just ripple over her skin but surged through every inch of her body like a rush of electricity or a mind-numbing drug.

Streaking her hands down his back, she held him tight as he pushed her close to the edge of orgasm. Shifting his stance, he gripped her butt cheek tighter, pressed her hard against the wall and buried himself so deep she swore she could feel him in her chest.

Gasping from the fierce assault on her flesh, she dug her nails in and raked them across his skin, happy when he cried out in pain and pleasure. Moaning loudly, she urged him on as she bucked and writhed against his body. He didn't disappoint but rammed into her harder and faster until she couldn't breathe and sweat dripped off them both.

She was so close to climaxing that every nerve and muscle in her body clenched. She felt faint and her eyes rolled back. She dug her fingers into his shoulders and bit her lip. She was there, so there. And it was going to be explosive.

Ronan nuzzled his face in her neck, and hefting her up, he drove hard between her legs. He shouted out her name, again and again, until she could feel him empty himself into her. Clamping her eyes shut, she cried out at her own orgasm.

They stayed like that, linked together, up against the wall, both breathing hard. Ivy could barely think past the heat of her body and the insistent throb between her legs. All her muscles felt like they'd melted into goo. She knew she wouldn't be able to stand if Ronan set her back on her feet.

Thankfully she didn't have to worry about that because he lifted her up, and turning, walked across the room with her straddling his waist, drew out of her and dumped her on the bed. He stepped back and looked at her with those penetrating eyes of his.

"Just give me a minute and we can try that again."

Laughing, she sat up, pulled her T-shirt off and tossed it onto the floor. "I'm ready when you are."

With a smile on his beautiful mouth, he tore at his own shirt, tossed it to the side and jumped onto the bed, wrapping his arms around her and rolling her onto the mattress. "Okay, I'm ready."

Chapter 27

For the next two glorious hours, they made love. Ronan didn't know he had that much stamina, but he figured it was because of Ivy. She pushed him to his limits in so many ways.

As the sun set, they lay on their sides in the bed under the covers, and he snuggled up against her back, spooning. He'd never been a fan of the spoon until now. He liked that he cradled her into his body, one hand pressed to her belly holding her tight, and could look down at her face while he played with her hair. He liked that he could see the twitch of her lips every so often when she thought of something amusing.

She was doing that now.

He ran a finger down her cheek. "What's funny?"

"How ironic life is."

"Yeah, who would've thought we would've ended up here together?" He tucked a stray hair behind her ear, and then pressed a light kiss to her head. "I thought for sure you would've tried to kill me more times than you already did."

She chuckled. "I only tried once."

"True."

"I may have thought about it a few times, though."

He laughed, and then tugged on the strand of hair he'd been wrapping around his finger over and over.

Sighing, she wriggled closer to him, her rear end brushing up against his groin. It didn't take long for Ronan to become aroused. She was like that to him. A drug. Just the softest touch of her could pump him full of adrenaline.

He nibbled on her ear. "You better stop that, or we'll be going for round three. Or is it four?"

"Four," she murmured, then yawned. "Save it for later. I'm too tired."

He chuckled. "I never thought I'd see the day when Ivy Strom was too tired for anything."

"Yeah, well, don't get used to it. It's been a long week." She closed her eyes, then grabbing his hand from her belly, she brought it up to her chin, tucking it there. "Give me about ten hours of sleep and I'll be good to go. Wherever you want to go. We should go on a holiday. We've both earned it."

"Sounds good," he whispered against her ear.

"I hear the Caribbean is cool."

"I like that."

"You'll be here when I wake up, right? We're going back home, together." She yawned again. "Besides, I need a place to stay. My safe house was destroyed. Your apartment is pretty big."

"Yeah, it's pretty big."

"Good, then that solves that problem."

Ronan had so many things to say, but he couldn't find the words to say them. He was a coward, plain and simple. For all his bravado, Ivy scared him in so many ways. She was stronger than him, inside. She had the fortitude of a steel giant. And the loyalty of a platoon of soldiers. He lacked all of that. His shame made his gut roil.

She slowly opened her eyes and looked at him, a soft, sleepy smile on her beautiful face. "You're my hero, Ronan. You keep saving me."

His throat constricted but he managed to say, "It's because I like you so much."

Her eyes fluttered closed, then she mumbled sleepily, "Yeah, well, I think I may love…" Her words trailed off as she fell asleep.

"I'm in love with you, too, Ivy Strom." He

pressed his lips to her temple, drinking her in, savoring each second he had with her. He knew too well how everything could change in a blink of an eye. How it was going to change.

He watched her sleep for an hour, smelling her, touching her skin, her hair, anything he could without waking her. Then, as carefully as he could, pulling his arm out from under her head, he rolled over onto his back and started planning.

The bright light streaming in through the dingy window stabbed Ivy in the eyes as she blinked them open. She closed them again. Shutting the light out and yawning, she rolled onto her back. She opened her eyes again and stretched, trying to work out all the kinks that had settled into her muscles. And there were a lot. From the past few days of fighting, and, well, from a hot session of awesome sex.

Thinking of sex, she turned her head to the side looking for Ronan. But he wasn't there beside her. He must've gotten up to eat, most likely. The man did have a healthy appetite. Except when she put her hand against the mattress, the spot was cool, as were the sheets, as if he hadn't been there for hours.

She sat up, swung her legs off the bed and stood. She searched the floor for her clothes. She found her pants and T-shirt and her ruined panties. Once she was dressed, she shoved the panties into her pocket to toss in the trash later. Opening the door, she padded out into the corridor toward the kitchen. She heard male voices.

But neither voice belonged to Ronan. Just Quinn and another guy, Pete, she thought, sat at the kitchen table drinking coffee, by the delectable smell.

Quinn smiled when he saw her. "Good morning. Well, afternoon." He got up and went to the stove. "Need some coffee?" He poured it into a cup and handed it to her.

She took it absentmindedly. "Where's Ronan?"

Quinn shrugged. "Thought he was still sleeping with you."

"No, he must've gotten up early."

Pete looked at her over the rim of his coffee. "I've been up for hours and I haven't seen him."

"Okay, thanks." She took her coffee with her as she went back to the little room where they had stowed their stuff. With one hand trembling, she opened the door. Her stomach was churning and she licked her lips to keep from getting sick.

Her duffel bag was on the floor just where she'd put it, closed and looking untouched. But Ronan's gear was gone. Instead, on the floor was a white envelope with her name scrawled across it.

She bent over and picked it up. She turned it over in her fingers, afraid to open it. Afraid of what was inside. No matter what words he put there, it wouldn't fix the withering agony inside her. It was quickly filling her to the brim.

With the envelope pinched between her trembling fingers, she shuffled back into the kitchen.

Quinn frowned at her. "What's wrong?"

"He's gone."

Her brother didn't say anything for a minute, just looked at her. "Maybe he had something to take care of. Did you read the letter?"

She shook her head, then put a hand up to her chest where her heart pounded so hard it felt like it was going to burst out from between her ribs and fall to the floor, ripped up and torn into shreds.

Then Quinn's frown deepened and he pushed to his feet. "Ivy? Where's your necklace?"

She looked down and ran a hand over her shirt, the pain in both her gut and her heart doubling. The necklace she never took off. The one she'd been wearing to bed. It was gone. Ronan had taken the key.

Chapter 28

Ronan paced the shoreline of the bay, waiting for Reginald and his cabal goons to show. The fog swirled around his boots like gray smoke. He'd told the sorcerer to come alone, but he knew that would never happen. Reginald was too much of a coward to come by himself. A coward. Ha, he should talk.

He'd snuck out of the farmhouse in Sumner like a thief in the night. Which was exactly what he was. He'd stolen the key, Ivy's precious necklace, from around her neck while she'd been sleeping. He'd quietly slipped from the bed, dressed, grabbed his gear, with the cross in it, and snuck out of the house. He'd hoofed it down to Main

Street and hot-wired a car, speeding down the highway back to San Francisco.

Now he held the key in his hand, fisted tight, while he waited for the man who'd paid him to acquire it.

Not for the first time, he had to swallow down the lump of guilt that kept coming up. His gut was constantly churning. He'd never felt this kind of remorse before. It was damn near killing him.

He'd almost not done it. He'd been lying there beside her, listening to her breathe, taking in her smell and the heat of her body next to him and he nearly just rolled over and forgot about the key and what it meant to him. He'd almost forgotten how many years he'd been searching for a cure. Almost.

Ivy meant a lot to him. He loved her. But the demon blood that ran through his veins would always come between them. It would be a constant bone of contention for them.

The irony of the fact that he had to steal the key from her, thereby ruining any chance of them being together anyway, wasn't lost on him. He understood the risks when he'd slipped the chain off her and slid it into his jacket pocket.

He just didn't realize it would hurt him so much to betray her.

Ronan stopped pacing and listened to the

sounds around him. The lapping of the water against the shore calmed his nerves a little. He'd always felt safe around water. The sounds and smell centered him, gave him a sense of peace. Something he was in desperate need of. He'd chosen this spot along the bay for that reason, and also because water dampened magic. He wasn't sure why; something about the living ions in water molecules. All he knew was it would prove to be difficult for old Reggie to zap him with some sinister spell so close to the water. That was a good enough explanation for him.

He pulled out his cell phone from his pocket and checked his messages for the tenth time since arriving back in the city. Still nothing from Ivy. This shouldn't have surprised him. What did he expect? Her declarations of love and anger over what he'd done to her? He should've expected silence from her. He'd just betrayed her in the worst way.

But he was hoping for a message, one that said she was coming to find him and kill him. He could handle that, maybe even would have pleasure in the fact that she cared enough to look for him. The silence ate at him. The silence was telling.

He shoved the phone back into his pocket just as he felt something stirring in the air. It wasn't the same sense he got when a demon was near, but it was close. Reginald Watson had arrived.

The sorcerer stepped out of the darkness and into a pool of moonlight. He gestured to the surroundings. "Interesting choice for a meeting."

"I like the water."

Reggie just smiled, but it wasn't one of friendliness; it held traces of arrogance and malevolence. The sorcerer knew exactly why he'd chosen this spot. The grin gave Ronan the creeps. He should've never gotten involved with the cabal. They were bad news.

Out of the corner of Ronan's eye, he spied two other sorcerers hiding in the shadows, one on either side. It was obvious Reggie didn't trust him, or in fact might just try and kill him when the transaction was done instead of giving him the cure.

"Do you have the key?"

Ronan nodded.

"Let me see it."

"I will, but first I want to know what you plan on doing with it."

Reggie frowned. "Why does that matter? You didn't care when you took the job."

"It matters now."

He stepped toward Ronan, his hands folded in

front. "What do you think we're going to do with it, Ronan?"

"Open the Chest of Sorrows and take Solomon's grimoire to release the demons."

Reggie chuckled. "You've been doing your homework." He pointed at Ronan. "Let me guess? Quianna Lang?"

Ronan didn't say anything.

The sorcerer shook his head. "She's always been meddlesome. Doesn't know her place."

"You can't control them," Ronan said.

"Of course we can. The cabal's power is limitless."

"I imagine Solomon thought that, too."

"Yes, well, he was one man. We are many. And we have been training for this for centuries. Now is the time to fulfill our destinies."

"You're delusional, Reggie. No one can control that many demons. Not even if there were one hundred of you. Which I know for a fact, there aren't."

He moved a little closer to Ronan. "There are enough of us not to be trifled with." He held out his hand. "Now, give me the key."

"I just have a few more conditions first."

"You're changing our arrangement."

"Yes, I am."

Reggie shook his head. "I don't like changes, Ronan. I really don't."

"First off, I want you to make a pact that you won't ever harm Quianna Lang. Or Ivy and Quinn Strom."

The sorcerer clapped his hands together and laughed. "Oh, dear boy. That's what this is about? Ivy Strom? You fell for that bitch. I can't believe it."

Ronan took a step toward him. "Better watch your mouth, Reggie, or I'll knock all your teeth out."

"Testy, testy. Doesn't look good on you, Ronan. I thought hellspawn didn't have feelings."

"I'm only half hellspawn." In a single second, he'd breached the short distance between them and grabbed Reggie around the throat, lifting him off the ground. "And our deal is off."

Reggie flung out his hands to the sides. Blue light ignited from his fingertips. Ronan could feel an electric sizzle in the air and knew he was about to get an enormous shock to his system.

He dropped Reggie and ran toward the water just as the other two sorcerers rushed out of the darkness. They also had blue sparks bubbling on their fingertips. Ronan drew his gun and fired on the one closest to him. The bullet grazed the sorcerer's arm. Crying out, he grabbed his arm. It was enough for the magic blue sparks to disappear.

Ronan swung around to the other one, but it

was too late. The sorcerer let go with a blast of magic. It hit Ronan in his left side. It was like being electrocuted. He dropped to one knee, gritting his teeth as pain shot through his body. Thankfully, the water had dampened the effects. He imagined that burst of magic should've stopped his heart.

The one sorcerer advanced on him, likely thinking he had put Ronan down. Pity for him. Ronan swung his gun up. This time he didn't miss. The bullet took the sorcerer in the gut and he dropped to the ground.

Ronan pushed to his feet and started for the water again. If he could jump in, he would be safe. He could hold his breath for a long time. Besides that, the cabal's magic couldn't touch him in the water.

As he sprinted, he could hear Reggie running behind him, his breath coming out in harsh pants. "You've doomed yourself for her, Ronan."

I know, he thought, *but she's worth it.*

A blast of magic erupted right behind him. Bits of dirt and rock hit him in the back of the legs. But he didn't slow.

"You'll never be human again. You've lost your one and only chance for a cure."

Another blast, this one a little closer. The blue bolt zipped across his right leg. It burned a hole in his pants. Luckily, it missed his skin.

He was a foot from the water's edge. Another blast came. This one grazed his left arm. Agony seared through him and he dropped. Right into the water.

Ronan pushed with his legs and went under. There was instant relief on his singed arm. He kicked hard and dove down deep. He swam out a ways, and then came up to the surface. He spied Reggie and his injured minion glaring out at him from the shoreline. He lifted his arm out of the water and gave them the finger.

"It doesn't matter, Ronan," Reggie shouted at him. "You've done all this for nothing. You'll never be with her, hellspawn. You think I'd let the Stroms live? They know too much. They are too much of a liability." Reggie's laughter echoed off the water's surface. "While you bob up and down in that water, my people are stripping the flesh off their bones."

Ronan's heart thumped hard and his gut roiled at the thought. But he didn't believe it. Both Ivy and Quinn were too smart and too careful to be ambushed by some cabal sorcerers. Still, dread filled him and he had to swallow down the fury that bubbled up inside him.

If he found this to be true, there would be no place for Reggie and his ilk to hide. Ronan would hunt them all down and kill them, nice and slow.

He had a lot of talent with a knife and oodles of patience.

Ronan turned and dove back down into the water. He had parked his stolen car about a mile down the shore in the event of something going wrong. Like it had. He would swim there, get in and find Ivy. Just to make sure.

Chapter 29

Ivy unlocked the front door of the old bungalow and walked into the foyer. It had been over two years since she'd been in the house. It was the house that Quinn and she had shared with their father before he died. After his death, she and Quinn had lived there until Quinn did a runner. Then she'd stayed for maybe a year before forging her own path into the demon-hunting world.

But it felt good to be back. She flicked on the hall light. Everything was as she'd left it. All the furniture had been covered with sheets. The place had a musty scent, though, but nothing some open windows and air freshener wouldn't cure.

She dragged her bags into the living room,

then dropped them onto the hardwood floor. She whipped off the sheet from the sofa and collapsed onto it. She was exhausted.

The trip back from Sumner was long, hard and trying on all her emotions. She'd driven straight through without any long stops. The only time she did stop was to use the facilities or to get coffee and food.

Quinn had asked her to come with him to track down Ronan. But she'd refused. He'd left in another vehicle intending to find the cambion and kill him. Ivy didn't want to be a part of that. No matter what Ronan had done, she couldn't see him harmed. Well, maybe just a little. But by her hands, and no others.

She didn't want to know what Quinn planned on doing. It was out of her hands. Her brother would do what he wanted. He would do what he had to, to retrieve the key. She understood that. The connection to honor and loyalty and a person's word. It had been ingrained in her, as well. Their father had been huge on doing whatever it took to do the job. The job was the most important thing. Nothing else mattered.

Ivy ran her hands over her face and sighed, leaning her head back on the sofa pillows. She used to think that, feel it, live it. But after meeting Ronan and falling for him, she realized that there was so much more than following a path, adhering to a code. There was great sex and love and all the messed-up crap that came with it.

She looked at one of her bags on the floor and reached over with her foot, hooked it and dragged it over. She unzipped it and took out the white envelope with her name written across it. She had yet to open it. She was afraid to.

What if Ronan took the key and left because he'd been using her this whole time? What if he truly didn't have any feelings for her? Then her ideas that she'd never truly been worthy of being loved would be confirmed. She didn't know if she could face that. Sometimes she liked her delusions. They were safe.

She tore open the envelope and slid out the plain white piece of paper. She unfolded it and read.

Ivy,
I could say I'm sorry, but I know that doesn't cut it. I imagine nothing would make what I did okay. To know that I have been searching for a cure for years, that I loathe the blood inside me, wouldn't be enough. But do know and believe this…
    That I didn't fall for you because of the key. I fell in love with you because of you.
Ronan

She read it twice, then crumpled it up into her fist and tossed it across the room. Tears stung her eyes and she was about to wipe them away when she heard a noise at her window.

She jumped to her feet and rushed to the big bay window. She pushed the drapes aside and looked out into the yard and onto the porch along the side. There was no movement. But she sensed someone was out there, watching her.

Unsheathing one of her blades, she moved to the front door, quietly turned the knob and stepped out onto the porch. A cool light breeze blew her hair around her head and over her face. She looked to the right and then to the left but didn't see any movement. A dog barked in the distance and she could hear the faint revving of a car engine nearby.

Then she spied it. A glint in the cypress tree in the yard. There was something hanging from one of the branches. Glancing around cautiously, Ivy stepped off the porch and crossed the lawn to the tree on the far corner.

Each step grew heavier and heavier as she drew closer to the tree. She knew what was hanging there and it formed a lump in her throat.

When she was right under the branch, she reached up and touched the thing hanging there. It was her cross necklace. It was the key.

She pulled it down, and gripping it tight in her

hand, she twirled around the yard. He was here somewhere. She knew he'd watch her retrieve it. She knew he'd been at the window watching her. She could always feel when his gaze was on her. It made gooseflesh rise on her skin.

"Ronan," she called.

A dog barked. Wind chimes tinkled somewhere nearby. But there wasn't any answer.

She returned to the porch, and instead of going back inside, she stood there and waited and watched. Maybe if she stood there long enough she would see him flit through the shadows. Maybe he would come to her, himself.

"Ronan," she called again. "I know you're there."

Still no answer. Just the rustling of the leaves in the tree.

But after an hour of standing there, her legs cramped and her stomach grumbled reminding her that she hadn't eaten in over eight hours. She went back inside, the key still clutched tight in her hand.

Ronan watched her go back into the house from his perch on the roof of the neighbor's place. He'd been tempted to go down and talk to her. She'd been waiting for him to, that was obvious. But he hadn't been ready, and neither had she. The anger of his betrayal would've still been fresh in her mind. She would've acted on it, he knew. And he really wasn't up to fighting with her. He was still sore from his encounter with Reggie and his cabal goons.

She was safe; that was all that mattered right now. Reggie had been lying about sending someone to take care of her. He should've suspected as much, but he had to be sure. The thought of something happening to Ivy, especially because of him, made his gut clench and his heart ache. He wouldn't be able to live with himself.

He also needed to give her time. Time to think, time to heal, time to forgive. He needed that time, too. To reconcile the fact that he'd never be fully human again. That he would always be a cambion, always have demon blood flowing inside him.

He had to see himself as Ivy had seen him.

As a man.

Until then, he wouldn't be good for her. And he really wanted to be good enough for her. She deserved that. She deserved the best he could be.

Once the door was shut and he heard the lock engage, he jumped down from the roof, walked down the street to his car and got in. He couldn't go back to his apartment. The cabal would be all over it. So this was his chance to make a clean break from everything he used to be. And be-

come someone different. Someone better. Someone worth Ivy's love.

But first he had to stop the cabal from doing
anyone else any harm.

Chapter 30

Ronan tossed the chalk to the side after drawing the sigil in the pentagram. He picked up his knife and drew the blade across his palm. Blood dripped onto the chalked hardwood floor of his newly rented apartment, activating the "call." It wouldn't be long before Daeva appeared. She was always prompt when he called her.

A minute passed before there was an audible pop and the scent of cinnamon filled the air.

"Hmm, twice in one week. That is some kind of record." Her grin was warm and friendly.

He didn't return the smile; this was all business. "I need another address."

"Well, I know it isn't for Sallos, because I saw

his sorry ass down here. You really pissed him off."

"I need to know the headquarters for the Crimson Hall Cabal."

Daeva tapped one long finger against her lips. "I see. That's quite the task you're asking of me."

"Why?"

"The cabal is powerful. They have a lot of magic able to block out any unwanted attention."

"I believe in you, Daeva. I wouldn't have called you if I didn't think you were the woman for the job."

She preened at his use of the word woman, instead of calling her a demon. He understood wanting that distinction. He lived it every day, as she did.

"Of course I am." She tapped at her lips again. "Give me some time."

"I need it sooner than later."

"It'll cost you."

Ronan looked at her, knowing full well that he'd pay whatever she asked for. He had to stop the cabal at any price. Reggie wouldn't quit until Ronan was dead, as well as anyone involved with the key. And that included Ivy and Quinn. Ronan would sacrifice his own life before he ever saw anything terrible happen to them.

"I know."

Daeva studied him for a moment, and then lifted one elegant eyebrow. "You're in love with her, aren't you?"

He dropped his gaze, uncomfortable with the way she saw right through him. "Does it matter?"

"Oh, Ronan, of course it does." She tsked, then snapped her fingers and disappeared.

Ronan walked down the corridor to the bathroom and stuck his hand under a stream of cold water. He kept it there until the blood oozing from the open wound gelled. He dried it carefully and then wrapped it up in gauze, taping it tight.

He didn't know how long he'd have to wait for Daeva to come back, but he sensed it wouldn't be too long. She was reliable and something in her eyes told him that she understood his feelings for Ivy. That somewhere and sometime she'd possessed those same feelings for someone.

True to his assumption, Ronan didn't wait long for Daeva's return. After two hours, she popped back into his living room with the information he needed.

She handed him a small piece of paper. He took it and said, "Thank you." He unfolded it, read the address, and then slipped it into his front jeans' pocket.

"That's why you called me."

"Name your price, and I'll pay it."

Daeva eyed him for a long while. So long he began to feel uncomfortable and shifted from foot to foot. Those gray eyes of hers were strange and unnerving. Finally she said, "All I ask is that you take care of her."

That surprised him. "What?"

"Look after Ivy Strom and love her like she deserves."

He still didn't get it. "That's all you want?"

She nodded.

"Why? What's Ivy to you?"

"Nothing. It's what she means to you." Then her eyes sparkled and a sly grin spread across her comely face. "Oh, and send a message to that brother of hers."

"What message?"

"That I'm waiting." Her eyes bled black, and then she was gone, in a puff of dark smoke.

Ronan didn't have time to dwell on that last bit about Quinn. He'd deliver the message sometime and let Quinn worry about it. Right now, he had to prepare to take down the Crimson Hall Cabal or at the very least, kill Reggie.

As soon as the sun set, Ronan set out on his way. The address Daeva gave him turned out to be smack in the middle of Pacific Heights. Not far from Lafayette Park, Ronan stood on Gough

Street and stared up at the huge Victorian mansion looming in front of him.

He shouldn't have expected anything less from the cabal. They were entrenched in money. Reggie alone was probably worth at least several million. Ronan imagined most of the cabal members came from wealth. Bunch of sorcerer snobs.

By looking at the big house, he also knew there were likely wards on every entrance. Luckily, Daeva also gave him the one window to go through that was lacking any security. He looked down at the paper she'd given him again. *Second story, third window from the right.* Smiling, he slid the paper back into his pants pocket and crossed the street.

Getting up to the second floor proved far easier than he thought it would be. Ronan slid open the unlocked windowpane and climbed into the dark room that just happened to be a bedroom. Reggie's bedroom, to be exact. And the sorcerer was sound asleep under the covers, like a gift-wrapped present.

But Ronan didn't believe in easy.

Pulling his gun out from his shoulder holster, he flicked off the safety. He aimed and fired off three rounds. All three bullets hit the sleeping form. The big problem was, no blood splattered from the holes.

A blast of magic hit him in the side. He stumbled to the left and smacked into the wall, the breath knocked out of him. His fingertips tingled from the electrical power of Reggie's magic.

"Did you think it would be that easy?"

"I was hoping," Ronan grunted, as he pushed off the wall and swung around to face his attacker.

Reggie stepped out of the shadows; his hands were alight with the glowing blue of his magic. He lifted them towards Ronan. "After I kill you, I'm going to torture and kill your girlfriend."

"No, I don't think so, Reggie." Ronan ran at the sorcerer full speed. As he moved, he unsheathed two blades from his back harness; he'd gotten one just like Ivy's.

Reggie was caught off guard at Ronan's attack and didn't have time to release his magic. They tumbled to the floor in a tangle of arms and legs. Reggie wrapped his hands around Ronan's neck, intending to strangle him with power. But Ronan had been quicker.

The sorcerer's eyes widened when he realized what had just happened. He looked down and saw that Ronan had buried both blades into his body, one in each side. Blood poured down his torso and onto the off-white carpet.

Ronan pushed away from the sorcerer and got

to his feet, pulling the knives out as he did. There was no way Reggie would survive.

"You shouldn't have threatened her. I might've let you live."

Reggie blinked up at him, then slowly his eyelids closed. Ronan sensed the moment the sorcerer died. A chill rushed through the room.

Wiping the blood off on the sheets, Ronan quickly made his escape from the room. He had a lot of work ahead of him. He had to efficiently and effectively erase every trace of himself.

Chapter 31

One month later

Ivy ran a hand over her new cross necklace, fidgeting as she waited at the bar. The day after she'd gotten back the key, she'd handed it over to Quinn, then promptly went out and bought herself a shiny new silver cross to replace it. As she played with it with her fingers, she knew it wasn't the same and never would be. In more ways than she wanted to admit to herself.

The cross had represented so many things to her. Quinn's love and abandonment. As well as Ronan's betrayal. And his attempt at redemption when he brought it back. Thirty days later and she still was waiting for him to show up at her door and apologize.

The bartender set down another drink in front of her. Soda and lime. She took a sip and spun on her chair to check out the place again. This was her first job since coming back from Sumner. Another bar. What was it with demons and bars? She supposed there were easier targets here. Mostly drunk, desperate women in this particular place. So, perfect for a male demon predator.

This one was a little different, though. He hadn't killed anyone, yet. He just got them drunk or stoned, took them out back and seduced them. He was a lust demon. Sex was how he got his energy, how he fed.

This one also supposedly had important information that Quinn needed. Something about the Chest of Sorrows. The chest that King Solomon had encased his grimoire in. Hence, her brother was across the room sitting at a little table in the corner, surveying the same crowd she was. Unfortunately they didn't have a clue what the demon looked like. They just had to be on the lookout for the signs, do a sweep, listen to their amulets and hopefully find the right one with the hellfire in his eyes.

It was strange doing a job with Quinn. They hadn't worked together since before he'd left over three years ago. But they'd easily fallen back into a rhythm. With Quinn telling her what to do again. She'd wanted to tell him to shove it up his butt, but the fight had quickly gone out of her and she'd done what he asked without a comment. He'd seemed surprised, but didn't question it.

Her fire was fizzling. There wasn't much in life that fired her up anymore. Even hunting was starting to lose its spark. She was seriously thinking about quitting and finding something else to do with her life. Something that would stop reminding her of Ronan.

She took another sip of her drink, and then set it down. The guy sitting beside her took the opportunity to slide in closer to her. "Hey, baby. Can I buy you a real drink?"

She didn't even turn to face him. His booze breath managed to hit her in the face anyway. "No, thank you."

He touched her arm. This, of course, was a huge mistake. "Come on. That's why you're here, isn't it? To hook up with someone like me?"

She turned, then, to look at him, about to tell him to take a flying leap off a high cliff, when the fire in his eyes froze the words in her throat. Her amulet was glowing blue and it burned her skin. She'd been so distracted that she hadn't noticed it warming on her flesh before now.

He grinned at her. "Hello, Ivy Strom. It's so awesome to finally meet you." Before she could react, he had her spun around and forced her into a headlock, a knife pricking at her throat. "Don't move or I will slice you open."

The other patrons around them jumped back and two lovely drunk ladies screamed at the top of their lungs. This was good, she supposed, because it would let Quinn know she was in some serious shit.

He started backing up, dragging her with him. Others moved out of their way, giving him fantastic access to the exit. She really wished people would sometimes get involved.

Quinn moved up along one side, but the demon spied him. Probably noticed him long before he even got there. The demon poked her in the neck with the tip of the blade. It stung something fierce.

"One more step, Quinn Strom, and baby sister here is dead."

Quinn put his hands up, palm out, in surrender. "Look, we just want to talk to you. We're not here to kill you."

The demon smirked. "Yeah, right. When have the Stroms not killed demons? You're famous for it." He continued to back up toward the exit.

Quinn followed him, careful of not getting too close to spook him. Thank goodness, because believe it or not the demon's hand shook. The tip of the blade pressed into her skin with every shake. He was afraid. That surprised her.

"I just have a couple of questions. I promise no harm will come to you."

The demon didn't believe him. Ivy didn't, either. She knew Quinn would put him down no matter what he told them. He was single-minded that way. He had a ferocious hate on for demons in all forms.

The demon snickered. "Yeah, right." They were a couple feet from the exit. A few people crowded around the door. "Open the damn door or I will cut this bitch open," the demon shouted.

One enterprising guy jumped up and ran to open the door for them. Ivy wanted to kick him in the balls on the way out. *Thanks for helping, buddy.*

Quinn followed them out, his hands still up. She knew he was looking for a way to take the demon down without getting her killed. She was pondering the same thing. But just swallowing was killing her. The demon was getting careless with his knife. Almost every step he took jogged his hand and nicked her skin. She'd bleed out soon enough if he kept it up because one of those careless nicks could get her right in the jugular.

Once they were outside, Ivy looked around, or as much as she could without turning her head.

She had to do something soon. She couldn't let him take her any farther, especially not into a waiting vehicle. This had to end now.

Although she couldn't see his face, Ivy knew the demon was also looking around, trying to figure out how he was going to escape unscathed. She could've told him that was an impossibility. After another minute, she sensed that he came to the same conclusion because she felt him relax a little.

"If I answer your questions, will you let me go?"

Quinn nodded. "Yes, but first you let my sister go."

The demon shook his head. "No, I think I'll keep her for a little while longer, just in case." He turned her head so she could look at his face. "You don't mind, do you, baby?"

She glared at him, and then croaked, "No, not at all, dickhead."

He chuckled, but it had a nervous twitter to it. "Ask your questions."

"Have you heard of the Chest of Sorrows?"

The demon shrugged, which caused his hand to move, which caused another slit along her skin.

"Watch your blade, asshole," Ivy barked.

"Oh, sorry, sugar." He lifted it slightly, enough that she considered her next move. He may have afforded her enough space between her neck and blade where she could safely break his hold on her.

"Was that a yes or no answer?" Quinn asked, his hand lowered to his sides now. It looked like he was gearing up to make a move, as well.

"I may have."

"Do you know where it is?"

"No. But I might know who does."

"Who?"

"Before I tell you, I want a guarantee I'll get out of here alive."

"I give you my word," Quinn said.

The demon shook his head. "Sorry, but somehow that doesn't give me any confidence." He backed up again, taking Ivy with him. "No, I'll just take pretty sis here with me until I think I'm safe, and then I'll tell you."

Quinn kept in step with them, about five feet away at all times. He looked at Ivy; she knew he was asking her the question, *Can you safely get away?* She didn't know for sure. The demon had a pretty tight hold on her, demons were megastrong and that lousy blade kept wavering dangerously at the main vein in her neck. If she made a mistake, moved too fast, went too slow, that tip could easily slide in and she'd be done for. She couldn't heal from something like that. If only Ronan were here, then maybe she'd consider it. He wouldn't let her die.

The demon kept backing up until he came to the street. There was an old sedan parked partially on the curb. He backed up to it, then smashed in the driver's-side window with his elbow. Reaching behind him, he opened the door.

"You first, little sister."

Ivy looked at Quinn for a cue. His eyes widened and then a little smirk grew on his face. What was he trying to tell her? Something was obviously going on.

"You just damaged my car, my friend. Big mistake." The deep voice vibrated over her and she closed her eyes in relief.

Next thing she knew, the demon was no longer holding her hostage. He was flying backwards over the car and out onto the street. Ivy swirled around to see Ronan standing on the roof of the car.

He jumped down, walked to the fallen demon, grabbed him by the shirt collar and dragged him back to the car. He pushed him up against the hood and slapped something on his chest. It was one of her devil's-trap stickers.

He caught her looking at it and shrugged. "You left some in my gear." He then motioned toward Quinn. "You can ask your questions now."

As Quinn moved forward, Ronan stepped away. Ivy wasn't surprised. He wouldn't know what Quinn would do. He did steal the key and all. Yeah, he brought it back, but in Quinn's eyes it didn't matter.

And did it matter to her? She didn't know. All she knew was that her heart thudded in her chest and her gut clenched when she looked at him.

He moved toward her, his steps hesitant. It looked like he'd bolt at a second's notice.

"Thanks," she said. "Again. For saving me."

He gave her a little smile. "Seems to be a habit of mine." He pointed to her neck. "You're bleeding pretty good there."

She touched her throat; her hand came away smeared in crimson. She could feel warm trickles sneaking under the collar of her shirt. "Yeah, he nicked me a few times too many."

He stepped even closer to her. She could smell him now. A dark, dangerous scent clung to him like shadows. "Let me see." He touched her neck with just his fingertips.

She shivered as a warm sensation drew over her throat, down her shoulders and ventured lower still. She felt her nipples harden instantly under her shirt. She stifled the urge to cover her breasts with her arm to stop him from noticing. It didn't matter. He noticed. She could tell by the slow, lazy smile that spread over his face and the gleam in his dark eyes.

He dropped his hand from her and took a step back. "There. The bleeding should stop."

She stared at him for a long moment, taking everything about him in. He looked the same. Maybe his hair was a little longer; the ends flirted with his earlobes. But he was the same. And in that moment she remembered every reason why she fell in love with him. Those reasons hadn't gone away.

"I like your necklace."

She reached up and stroked a hand over the silver cross. "At least it's just a cross."

His lips twitched a little. "Yeah, good thing, that."

"I gave the key to Quinn."

"I figured you would. It's best with him anyway."

"Why did you bring it back?"

He looked at her, as if memorizing every nuance on her face, every line, every slope and every muscle. "Because being human meant never having a chance to be a man with you."

Her heart skipped a beat in her chest and she had to fight down the urge to let the tears welling in her eyes fall. Instead, she cleared her throat and kicked at a small pebble on the ground. "Quinn won't ever forgive you. I can't promise you that he won't try to kill you later."

"I don't care." He reached for her hand and took it in his. "All I need to know is…can you forgive me?"

Her skin warmed in his, and the sensation crept over her wrist and up to her biceps. He was doing that thing he knew she liked, when he transferred some of his power into her. It was sneaky, but she couldn't stop the giddiness inside her stomach. It was one more thing she liked about him.

"I don't know. Maybe in time."

"Good." He lifted her hand to his mouth and pressed a kiss on the back, and then he let her go. He turned to leave.

"Where are you going?"

"Giving you that time." He gave her one of his devilish smiles and walked out into the night, the shadows along the street swallowing him up.

Chapter 32

The jerk, she thought. He'd done it to her on purpose.

Every night for the past week since seeing him on the street in front of the club, she'd been waiting for him to show up at her house.

She would eat dinner, watch some TV, dress for bed then sit in her dark bedroom waiting for the knock at the door or at the window. It wouldn't have even surprised her if he slipped into the house unseen and unheard to take her by surprise.

But he hadn't shown and she was growing more impatient and frustrated with every passing minute.

Just the way he wanted her, she suspected.

She could've called him on his cell phone, but she didn't want to seem desperate. She didn't want him to have the upper hand. She was supposed to be trying to find ways to forgive him, when in reality she'd forgiven him the second she'd seen the hanging necklace glinting in the moonlight. She would've welcomed him back into her arms gladly.

Tonight, she'd met Jake for some prep on a new job. He'd had information she needed. He'd also informed her that the Crimson Hall Cabal was after her and to watch her back. Once they'd met, they'd talked, had a drink, then she'd left with Jake's warning fresh in her mind.

Jake hadn't asked her about Ronan, but she could tell he'd wanted to. Maybe it was the angry glare she'd given him when he started to open his mouth. Or the sadness that she couldn't stop from enveloping her when she thought no one was looking.

She'd had no real idea how truly empty her life was until Ronan had come into it and messed it all up. And now that he was gone, she felt not just empty but hollow. Like he'd taken all the good stuff with him.

She parked her newly acquired vehicle in the carport, turned it off and got out. She was tired and thought about nothing but climbing into bed and sleeping. She slipped inside and locked the door behind her. She toed off her sneakers and padded across the living room toward her bedroom with every intention of stripping off her clothes and sliding under the sheets.

But the second she stepped into her dark bedroom, she sensed something was wrong.

She unsheathed a blade from her back harness and held it out defensively. Her breathing slowed and she tilted her head to hear. A rush of movement came from her right, and she swung her arm but it was blocked. She was grabbed around the biceps and pushed up against the bedroom wall. A warm sensation stroked her skin.

She growled, "What took you so damn long?"

Ronan smiled. "I was giving you time to forgive me."

"Yeah, well, time's up buddy." She dropped her knife, and wrapped her hand around his neck, pulling his mouth even closer. "Kiss me before I change my mind."

He did. And it was good.

A rush of delicious shivers raced down her spine. Her other hand found purpose under the hem of his shirt, as she feathered her fingers over his stomach and up to the hard planes of his chest. He moaned into her mouth as she rolled one of his nipples between her fingers.

"Damn, woman, you're killing me."

"Get used to it," she said as she licked along his jawline. "I plan to kill you for a long time."

"Promise?"

She looked up at him, met his gaze, saw the question there and the answer. "Yes, I promise."

"Good, because waiting for you has been torture."

"Torture?" She nipped at his chin. "You're the one who was torturing me. Saying you'll give me time. You knew I would be waiting for you to show up. Not knowing if you would."

He laughed. "I thought that was what you loved about me. My unpredictability."

"Maybe."

He released her one arm, then cupped her face in his hand and looked into her eyes. "It's okay to say it, Ivy. It's okay to love me. Because I love you." He brushed his lips against hers. "For as long as I live, demon blood and all, I will love and protect you."

"I don't care about the demon blood, Ronan. You are more human to me than any other man has ever been. I love you, all of you, because of how you chose to use the power it's given you."

He found her mouth with his and kissed her hard and long. It had her head swimming by the time he was done. He released her other arm, then streaked both his hands down to her behind. He picked her up effortlessly and carried her across the room to the bed. He tossed her onto the mattress.

He started to strip off his T-shirt, pulling it up over his head. Ivy perched up onto her elbows to enjoy the show. He smiled as his fingers worked at the zipper of his pants, and he slowly pulled it down to reveal he'd gone commando.

"What about Quinn and the rest of the hunter community?" he asked.

"Screw them. I don't care. They'll just have to deal with it. Besides, you're a better hunter than most of them, so they should be thanking me for letting you hang around."

"Letting me hang around?" He quickly zipped up his pants. "Hmm, I think I'm insulted."

This had Ivy scrambling to the edge of the bed, grabbing for him. "Where are you going? You can't just tease me like that."

She tugged at his hips, pulling him closer to her. When he was situated right in front of her, she slowly unzipped him again.

"You're just using me for my extremely awesome body."

"Yeah, duh."

Laughing, he pushed her back onto the mattress and after quickly shedding his pants, he covered her body with his. He wrapped a hand in her hair. "Okay, you can use me for a while. But then I get to use your extremely hot body for the rest of your life."

"Deal."

With one mighty yank from his hand, her clothes were in pieces on the floor. He covered her mouth with his before she could protest and kissed her with every ounce of passion inside him. This was beyond anything she'd ever experienced. Or ever wanted to.

* * * *

Wrap up warm this winter with Sarah Morgan…

Sleigh Bells in the Snow

Kayla Green loves business and hates Christmas.

So when Jackson O'Neil invites her to Snow Crystal Resort to discuss their business proposal… the last thing she's expecting is to stay for Christmas dinner. As the snowflakes continue to fall, will the woman who doesn't believe in the magic of Christmas finally fall under its spell…?

4th October

www.millsandboon.co.uk/sarahmorgan

She's loved and lost — will she ever learn to open her heart again?

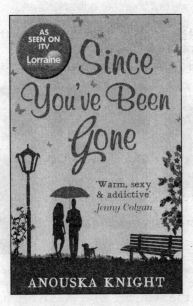

From the winner of ITV Lorraine's Racy Reads, Anouska Knight, comes a heart-warming tale of love, loss and confectionery.

'The perfect summer read — warm, sexy and addictive!'
—Jenny Colgan

For exclusive content visit:
www.millsandboon.co.uk/anouskaknight

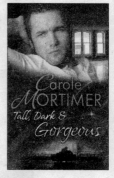

Join the Mills & Boon Book Club

Subscribe to **Nocturne**™ today for 3, 6 or 12 months and you could **save over £50!**

We'll also treat you to these fabulous extras:

- 🌹 FREE L'Occitane gift set worth £10

- 🌹 FREE home delivery

- 🌹 Rewards scheme, exclusive offers…and much more!

Subscribe now and save over £50
www.millsandboon.co.uk/subscribeme

What will you treat yourself to next?

Ignite your imagination, step into the past...
6 new stories every month

INTRIGUE...

Breathtaking romantic suspense
Up to 8 new stories every month

Captivating medical drama – with heart
6 new stories every month

MODERN™

International affairs, seduction & passion guaranteed
9 new stories every month

n o c t u r n e™

Deliciously wicked paranormal romance
Up to 4 new stories every month

Fresh, contemporary romances to tempt all lovers of great stories
4 new stories every month